Savage Love

Also by Douglas Glover

FICTION

The Mad River

Precious

Dog Attempts to Drown Man in Saskatoon

The South Will Rise at Noon

A Guide to Animal Behaviour

The Life and Times of Captain N.

16 Categories of Desire

Elle

Bad News of the Heart

NON-FICTION

Notes Home from a Prodigal Son

The Enamoured Knight

Attack of the Copula Spiders

DOUGLAS GLOVER

Savage Love

stories

Edited by Bethany Gibson.
Dust jacket and page design by Julie Scriver.
Dust jacket image: "Wolf vomit from my eyeballs," copyright © 2009
by Meagan Jenigen, www.thelostfur.com.
Endpaper design by StroomArt.
Printed in Canada.
10 9 8 7 6 5 4 3 2 1

Library and Archives Canada Cataloguing in Publication

Glover, Douglas, 1948-, author
Savage love / Douglas Glover.

Short stories.
Issued in print and electronic formats.
ISBN 978-0-86492-901-3 (bound). ISBN 978-0-86492-779-8 (epub)

I. Title.
PS8563.L64S29 2013 C813'.54 C2013-902182-5
C2013-902183-3

Goose Lane Editions acknowledges the generous support of the Canada Council for the Arts, the Government of Canada through the Canada Book Fund (CBF), and the Government of New Brunswick through the Department of Tourism, Heritage, and Culture.

Goose Lane Editions
500 Beaverbrook Court, Suite 330
Fredericton, New Brunswick
CANADA E3B 5X4
www.gooselane.com

For my sons, Jacob and Jonah, stout fellows.

"Stout fellow, the highest honour that can be bestowed on man or beast."

—P.C. Wren, *Beau Geste*

PRELUDE

FUGUES

INTERMEZZO
MICROSTORIES

THE COMEDIES

PRELUDE

Dancers at the Dawn

Moonlight illuminates the dancers and the whitewashed concrete bird bath by the standpipe, the coiled green garden hose, the liquid amber gum tree, and the tree nursery under the chicken-wire frame that keeps out rabbits and deer.

Phoenix Prill, the girl from hospice, says insomnia is a symptom of a morbid and excessive fear of death.

I say, "How could any fear of death be excessive? What would be the sense of a tempered fear of death? Perhaps, like everyone else, I should look forward to death and sleep well? Do you sleep well?" I ask her.

"No," she says.

Phoenix Prill has a tiny, iridescent mole on the inside of her thigh. It reminds me of an astronomical black hole, or perhaps the universe as it existed just before the Big Bang. It makes no sense, I believe, to say something existed just before the Big Bang, before the beginning of time. But Phoenix Prill invites paradox, and of course, the throw of language is deceptive. It's much better for describing things that don't exist than for pinning down reality.

No one else sees them. They come in the bowels of the night when I am sleepless—gibbering, howling beasts dancing on the lawn. One, a female, is dressed like a human in a white Communion frock burst at the seams. She writhes and twists in attitudes of erotic abandon, offering her backside to the males.

FUGUES

Tristiana

1869, Lost River Range, Idaho Territory

Against the winter he had scrupled not to lay in a sufficiency before the snow dropped. The snow surprised him. Snow choked the passes, interred the arid creek beds and dry washes under a mortuary sheet, muffled the canyons to the pine tips, buried his traps, buried his hut, his pole barn, his stock. He started by killing the lambs, stuffing their skins in the cracks between the sappy logs. Then he kilt the ewes, one by one, then he kilt the ram, then he kilt the ox and the riding mule, which was starving also. Then he kilt his wife. And then his dog, regretting of the dog more than the rest because it was a pure Tennessee Plott hound. Then he resigned himself to death, composed his body beneath a pile of frozen sheepskins in a corner, and waited. He wasn't defeated, he told himself, only indignant at the sudden wolfishness in the weather, which had descended without warning in the prospectus of his westward dreams. Yet it was imperative to die because of his losses and the embarrassment of curious bones lying about, of which the spring thaws would require an explanation.

Blue Girl

But he did not die, despite the wishing of it in the anguish of the famine pangs. One day he woke to splinters of hot sunlight piercing the log crevices. He had been dreaming of the cornfield where he stood with Hood's Texians in the storm of lead that in the dream resembled winter sleet whispering among the cornstalks, corpses gathering like drifts in the lees and gullies. He crawled to the door, which, for several hours, resisted his efforts to swing open he was that weakened and without purchase on the material world. Then he lay on the doorsill, half in, half out, absorbing the heat from the sun, water drops pocking down from the overhang, his tongue catching the drops. All the time regretting his furious, implacable and unthinking desire to live, which under the circumstances seemed to issue from an instinctive malevolence, a spirit of meanness.

The next morning, he crawled to the door again and licked mud. Dry, warm westerlies whistled up the valley like dragon's breath, eating snow. Along the mountainsides branches sprang back and reared, released from the burden. He sat with his back to the wall and tried to plumb the blinding, gleaming white world stretched before him. He saw something moving in the gleam, a dark, silhouetted thing struggling afoot in the treacherous element, then pitching forward and struggling up again, finally swaying upright, rooted in the snow. Thar's food, he thought, smacking his scabbed lips.

He wormed his way over the drifts, not trusting to put a foot down lest he anchor there and die, the impulse that kept him from dying so thin that like the crust of snow it barely held him up. When he got close, he could see it was a girl, just breasted, in nothing but a filthy smock, rusty stains down the front and a shit-tail from sickness down the back, bare arms and legs. Unthinkable where she came from, how she had come. He thought, when he thought, there was no one less than fifty miles away in these mountains, save for Indians. She was blue from the cold, deep-dyed blue that looked like it would never come out. Dead blue eyes, lacking brows and lashes, like slate bolts, yellow hair, and pox craters like a star constellation on her cheeks and brow.

He dragged her down beside him. "Lie on the crust," he said, though she seemed not to hear. He jerked his head this way and that, thinking there must be others, that she had strayed from a party nearby, but he saw no one. Her tracks walked away over the rise and disappeared. He touched her blue hand. It seemed solid, seemed to suck the heat right out of him. He tried to worm backwards, dragging her by the shoulders, but her feet held solid in the snow. He spent two hours digging and trying not to die till they came free. Bare feet, swollen and black with frost. Black to the ankles, where they turned blue by grades, hard as bricks. He glanced at her eyes wondering if she had an inkling of her condition, saw outright terror there, abject, infinite. "D'ye feel anythin'?" he asked. She shook her head once, side to side. "Yer won't last long," he said. "I got nothin' for ye. Are ye frightened of me?" he asked. She nodded. "Ye should be," he said. "Ye should be." He touched her flank. "I might breakfast of ye come mornin'."

The Hunt

She struggled wanly on the journey home but had not much fight after he struck her and let him drag her through the door, where she shamelessly let go and wet the packed earth floor. He said, "Ye might have done that ere we come inside. Ye had plenty of time." He piled his wife's last clothing and her wool coat over the girl, then crawled under with her and dragged sheepskins over their heads and fell unconscious until her shrieks bore him to the surface again. She was suffering the return of blood to her extremities like fire in the veins, like being consumed in the fire, writhing and clutching at herself till he clubbed her with an axe butt to subdue the noise. Then he could not sleep again but sat up shivering in the mule blanket, with bleared eyes eyeing the limp convexity of her form beneath the sheepskins in the trickle of moonlight that filtered through the walls.

Again the sun woke him, which in and of itself kept him alive a few more hours. He went out and ate mud. The girl did not stir, perhaps already dead. He found a stone and lounged in the morning light beside the door honing the axe blade, stopping every few passes to rest, but resolute, patient. He sharpened his butcher knife. The work warmed him. Then he was suddenly alert, cocking an ear for a sound he had not yet heard but sensed in the gelid stillness. Presently he heard it closer, the frenzied, high-pitched whimper and yip of a pack working its prey, wolves hunting beyond the rise. He crawled inside and unwrapped his Sharps rifle, pocketed a dozen linen cartridges and priming caps, then wrapped the rifle again in oilcloth and canvas and went out into the sunlight with it. The pack was closing. He could tell from the rising excitement of their mutual conversation.

He set out over the drifts, squirming along the worm trail he had left the day before and thence following the girl's track, dragging the rifle on a line tied to his belt. He like to have died there, crawling, the snow melting against his clothes, soaking him to the skin. He licked snow to wet his lips, blew on his red hands. Said to himself, Don't die, fuckwit. You survived the cornfield for this? Then he caught sight of the racked, plunging form of the elk, black and urgent against the brilliant, dazzled snow, tongue full out, eyeballs rolling white out of their sockets, dogs hanging off its hinders, ripping the tendons like bits of string, others circling, snapping and plunging themselves through the snow crust, floundering exhausted. All alike frenzied, half dead from winter rations, from the chase, all expressing alike the dumb, obstinate, ineluctable, violent will to stay alive.

He unlimbered the Sharps, tamped the canvas over a mound of snow in front of his face for a rest, cracked the breech, inserted a cartridge and fitted a cap over the nipple, rested the barrel on the canvas, flipped the rear sight up, and took cognizance of the distance and windage as best he could. He had not sighted in the gun since the snow fell and had no trust in his aim but squeezed off a round that by luck took a wolf in the rear near the spine. She tumbled, tried to rise, commenced worrying her own flanks with her teeth, snapping and snarling. The rifle report thundered off the valley walls. Whimpering with puzzlement, the she-wolf dragged her useless back legs, still trying to run the elk but falling over every step until the others turned on her, ripping her open in a fury of bared teeth, liquid snorts, gouts of blood, fur and entrails gobbled down and forgotten in the lust for more. A banner incarnadine in the snow.

He doggedly cleared the breech, reloaded and squeezed the trigger again, having an easier shot with the wolves bunched together like that, and wounded another, which, not being crippled, drew the others off a way in a running battle before he too succumbed. The elk tossed its antlered head and reared, attempting to pivot on its hind legs and escape along its old track, but was played out, short of blood and gripped fast in snow up to its belly, its nostrils venting gusts of pink steam, flanks heaving, and still nothing solid to fetch its hooves upon, only sinking deeper with its struggles.

He squirmed forward over the snow, excited now, sweating with the effort and exhilaration of the hunt, trembling with eagerness and anxiety lest this opportunity slip away, would have kilt more wolves to fend them off if he weren't husbanding his cartridges, the pack now watching him, panting heavily, raising a cloud over the gleaming rib cage of the dead one, muzzles lowered with exhaustion, wary of the human. He scrabbled desperate toward the elk, dragging himself on his elbows till he was near enough to touch the flank, then rose to a stand for the first time, sinking straightway up to his thighs but not stopped by it, thrashing up the length of the body from behind and driving his butcher knife into the animal's neck, searching with it for an artery, licking the hot, steaming blood off his hand where it came out in spurts as the elk expelled a breath and subsided in the snow, still breathing but gone.

He wept for thankfulness and set up his gun again toward the pack, which hung back but tracked with precise accuracy every movement he made. The shadows were lengthening, the dark line of the western ridge would shortly cut him off from the sun. He summoned every bit of pent-up strength and sawed the belly open along the rib line and reached in, warming his arm in the cavity, dragging out ropes of guts and reaching in again, rummaging around till he found the heart and tugged, feeling the arteries part, and he ate of it in the last sunlight, sucking out the blood, hot as if from a fire, and felt it flow into him like an inner light.

He put the heart in his coat and fumbled for the liver and hacked off the tongue, then, resurgent, separated the back legs and haunches at the hip, threaded lines between cannon bone and tendon, and knotted them to his belt, knowing they were too much for him but also knowing the wolves would devour everything he left. Then, letting himself down, he commenced the long crawl back to the hut, dragging the rifle and meat like sea anchors, not looking behind because he could not bear the thought of the wolves feasting on his kill, hurrying as best he could against the cold settling with the twilight, sweating inside his wet clothes but his breath freezing in his nostrils, his hands stiff and painful. Stop and die, he thought. You stop and you die. Darkness falling, stars appearing, moon shadows, wolf howls so close he felt himself enclosed in the mournful circle of their threnody.

Feet

In the morning, they were both took by the gripes from gorging on raw meat. The sun found them squatting against the wall, side by side, clutching their bellies, grunting to void, though nothing came. He said, "This will bring on the piles somethin' fierce." Then he said, "I will call ye Good Luck on account of it was good luck that brought ye to me and then it was good luck for ye that I shot that elk. But I expect that is the entire extent of yer good luck." He looked at her feet, which were beginning to fester and stink, jelly breaking through cracks in the skin. The colour edging up her ankles. "Do they pain ye?" he asked. She shook her head. Her buttocks were white and lean, he could see the mute line of her pussy in the mouse hairs. Under the filthy shift she looked quite clean, but her rank scent was strong in the close room where they slept.

He tore up part of the pole barn and made a fire in the dooryard and roasted strips of elk for breakfast. The spring sun was so hot it rebuked the months of his arctic entombment, as if it could not have been. He unwrapped the Sharps and reamed out the barrel, then he found his stone and honed the butcher knife again. "Good luck, good luck," he muttered as he worked. Around about, scattered bones, cracked and chewed for the marrow, began to work their way out of the snow like memories he would rather forget floating to the surface in a bad dream. The girl fell asleep in the sunlight wearing his wife's wool coat. Her blackened feet looked like something stuffed and inhuman, like feet she was wearing over her feet. And like the snow, they were beginning to melt.

"I hain't got a bone saw," he said, waking her with his boot. "But I seen them do this plenty after the cornfield fight. Some survived. Yer want me to put ye out?" He raised a fist. The girl shook her head, leaned back against the wall and pulled the coat tight over her breast. He braced one leg on a split rail, pounded into the mud flat side up, then he gave her a length of check line doubled up to bite on and marked a spot where the flesh was still white and healthy, and without forewarning made a quick, deep cut to the muscle, first one side, then the other, till they came together. Then he sliced up her shin toward her knee a good four inches and peeled the skin back like a sock. He had rehearsed it in his mind and so did not hesitate or falter, nor did the amount of blood leaking from the meat cause him to worry or flinch. He cut deeper to the bone and peeled back a sleeve of muscle and fat. Then he stepped back and hefted the axe, took one slow aiming stroke, then swung it above his head and down so strong that it cut the bone and halfway through the rail. Then he snatched a flaming log from the fire and clapped the red to the stump of her leg and held it till the sizzling ceased. He had needle and thread ready, dropped to his knees and methodically sewed the sleeve of muscle over the bone tip, then the flap over the stump. It had taken him twenty minutes, working in a tranquil frenzy. He had thrown his coat off in the heat of it and still dripped with sweat, trembled with fatigue after the intensity of effort.

He glanced at the girl for the first time since beginning. She was gone in a dead faint, eyeballs rolled up in her head, lids half closed, the check line fallen upon her breast halfway chewed, blood seeping from her lip where she had bitten through, fists clenched white, and an excavation of mud and snow where she had kneaded in her agony. He made to slap her then thought better of it, dropped his ear to her breast and, satisfied that she was still alive, turned his attention to the other foot while she could not feel the pain. Sliced, peeled, chopped and sewed, and checked to see that the first stump was not bleeding nor swelling. Then he stretched exhausted before the fire and dragged his coat over his head and slept till the cold woke him, shadows lengthening. The girl was staring at her legs and the feet where he had left them. Eyes like plates, repellent in their nakedness. And her strange silence that was getting on his nerves. "Yer might live now," he said, "if you've a mind to." But she seemed not to hear.

Boots for Good Luck

A spring blizzard let down overnight. The girl clung to him with a fierce desperation, shivering in gusts beneath the sheepskins, shaking him from unruly dreams. He did not expect nor hope that she would live, only regarded the matter with a distant circumspection as somewhat subordinate to his own preoccupation with survival. You stop and you die, he thought. Between that thought and the girl tormenting him he slept but little, and rose early to piss but could not get through the door so pissed in a corner against the wall. He chewed cold roast elk for breakfast in the dark and, fortified, broke through the drift in the doorway and kicked the fresh snow till he found his cache of firewood poles. He managed to light a smoky fire on the stone hearth in the room where they slept, but the chimney would not draw and smoke presently filled the room. In a rage, he kicked the door off its hinges and threw the door bits onto the fire and fanned the smoke out the doorway, which was not much help, and finally subsided beside the girl in the smoke and gloom, his heart murderous with frustration and desire.

He took to whittling with his pocket knife. He found an unsplit cylinder of pine and began to shave it down. The girl opened her eyes and he told her where to piss. She crawled on her hands and squatted on all fours, pissing backwards like an animal. Then he said, "Take off that rag. It stinks to heaven." She dragged her shift over her head and he threw it on the fire. Naked, on hands and knees, with no feet behind, she looked inhuman but not animal either, just alien, strange and mute. And yet she had some inner strength, a power of intention, with which he felt a kinship. What she had already endured he could not fathom. It did not matter if you were puny or strong, he thought, wrong or right; if you had the will, you could endure—until Fate or old age cut your string. Most just rolled over for the knife. He had seen it in the cornfield. He despised anyone who let himself die or whined, bargained, begged or prayed. He gave Good Luck his wife's last dress to cover her nakedness and cut and wrapped sheepskins around her stumps to keep her warm. She moved away from him, curled up close to the fire, and slept.

They were blockaded inside for a week, till he thought maybe winter had come back for good. They roasted the last of the elk, boiled the hooves, bones and sinews, scraped the hair off the skin, cut it up and boiled it and cracked and sucked the bones. He whittled the whole time because he had to be doing something, and at the end of the week had the semblance of a foot, an ankle and part of a leg, with a deep bowl cut and polished at the top to take her stump. He carved the toes and nails and little creases where the toes crooked, a dainty girl's foot, almost real in the firelight and smoke; it gleamed golden-red in the firelight. He checked her stumps every day for signs of putrescence, but they healed steadily, dry wounds with purple scar tissue pouting like lips and two rows of punctures where the thread sutures went in and out.

At the end of the week, the wind turned from the west again and a real spring thaw commenced, brutal and swift. Across the valley a cliff face of ice and rock let go and came rushing down in a thunderous wave. A freshet ran through the hut, and they had to sleep nigh to the wall, practically on top of one another, to stay dry. The new snow melted faster than the old, and he walked out one morning with the Sharps to see if any of his elk remained. All he could find was the upturned rib cage like the skeleton of an ancient wreck left high and dry by the tide and some long bones and vertebrae scattered about. He trudged over the lip of the next rise where he could see clear to an oddly feminine lithic cleft that boxed the head of the narrow valley. And just there, instead of game, he spied a thin column of smoke like an exclamation mark over a diamond of spruce trees nestled between two fans of scree with a flat, snowy expanse of pond in front.

He bent low and hastily retraced his steps out of sight, not because he was afraid but because he preferred to make his moves in secrecy, unencumbered by the complicity or anticipation of others. Home again, he kicked out the fire and thenceforth lit it only at night, blocking the door, smoke or not. They were starving again, but were used to that. Good Luck slept with her new foot held to her chest like a dolly. He feverishly commenced work on the other, carving doggedly while perched on a granite outcrop uphill from the hut, where he repaired every morning with the Sharps to keep watch.

The second foot came into shape faster than the first but without the niceties, just the notion of a foot that still looked like a piece of dead pine with the toes and nails scratched in to give an idea. The night he finished it, he dug in his traps for his spare boots, worn-out stove pipes with pegged soles and straight lasts for walking that he had after the war. He stuffed the new feet into the boots then wrapped Good Luck's stumps in lambskin and helped her pull the boots on till she was lodged firmly inside the wooden cups. He cut down the market straps from the mule harness and buckled them around the boot tops till they cut into the flesh below her knee, and said, "Stand." And then he said, "Walk." But she could do neither except she climbed her hands up the log wall and swayed in the doorway holding the jambs. "Walk," he said, but when she tried, her legs gave way for the tenderness in her stumps and general lack of use.

He knelt and rebuckled the market straps, tighter than before. Then he nudged her with his toe and said, "Get up, or you'll have another name." She started to drag herself up by the log wall, but he yanked her back, tossing her in a heap where the meltwater oozed. "Do it by yerself," he said. Again he was struck by how alien she seemed, on all fours, her lank, unkempt hair over her face, her lean amphibian torso dripping water, the big, ungainly boots gleaming dully behind like a tail. Something inhuman, indomitable, but veiled. She puked between her hands, wiped her mouth with a sleeve, then hitched one booted foot under her hips, rested her weight on it a moment, then hitched the other one, rested there, gathering her strength, then pressed herself up on her fingertips and pushed off. Not enough the first time, nor the second, but the third time she rose awkwardly above her feet into a stand. She kept her eyes on the floor. He could detect no aura of emotion save for the intensity of effort and concentration. She rocked a little one way and then the other, then slid the off foot forward an inch or two, and then the other.

The Easiest Prey

After the cornfield, the colonel put him in a sharpshooter company on the evidence of the quantity of Union dead along his front. He shot ten-inch patterns with a Leonard target rifle at two hundred yards and five hundred yards, and they issued him an English Whitworth with a four-power telescopic sight that cost a thousand dollars and could kill a man a mile away. He played cat and mouse with the Union artillery till the end of the war, mostly alone because he was a marked man, the Union gunners reaching out with percussion shells any time they had an inkling where he might be. Their officers had field glasses and watched for the muzzle flash. He never shot three times from the same stand. He ate alone, slept alone, and was let off drill and fatigues so he could perform his solitary duties in his own time. He shot officers, gunners, horses, mules, oxen, suttlers, drovers, niggers, dogs, and once set off a powder wagon. The Whitworth threw a hexagonal bullet that whistled eerily in flight and thus announced itself. He loved to watch a gun crew suddenly go still with dread, faces turning up like leaves, waiting to see who among them had been chosen. The colonel said, "You'un must've been whelped with a long gun in your hands." And then he said, "The easiest prey of all is a human nine hundred yards away and no knowledge of your presence, your gaze. If it weren't war, they'd call it murder." In December 1864, he went into winter quarters with the 1st and 4th Texas between the roads to Williamsburg and Charles City outside Richmond. One night he stole a wool coat from a drunk Irishman pressed for a work battalion, tossed the Whitworth into the James River, and deserted.

Before dawn, he made up two packs for himself and the girl, everything they could carry on their backs. He told her to stand, and she did. He said, "We'll leave by and by. Tonight or tomorrow. You best practise." He took a handful of the linen cartridges and the Sharps in its wrapping and slipped through the doorway before the sun came up. He kept to the timberline, not venturing into the open sage and grass ridges leading down to the narrow flats at the valley floor, and when the sun came up, he stepped back into the trees where the going was tedious and slow but where he was invisible. The snow was still deep amid the trees, the crust softened so he fell through time and again. He had to navigate deadfalls and rock slides and ford meltwater freshets that crashed down from the icy summits, flooding gullies. When he grew cold from the wet, he trudged faster to keep warm, and then he sweated from the effort and threw off his coat, rolled it and tied it over his shoulder, always suffering the discomfort, despising the exhaustion that now and again staggered him.

At length he met a rock spine going down with a crest of windblown evergreens like a coxcomb on top threaded by a game trail that was easy walking. He did not stop but let the trail lead him steeply down into the valley, unlimbering his rifle as he went, dropping the block, loading a cartridge, setting the cap and trimming the sights. He stopped before the trees thinned out completely and went to cover where he could see across the valley, steep-sided with islands of sage and hardy high desert grass and occasional hummocks with a few conifers holding their own, the meltwater eroding the lava dust in curves and fans, flooding the low ground and the pond and a creek emerging there and zigzagging lazily in the direction whence he had come. Smoke billowed from the camp, a freshly lit fire burning the damp off the tinder. He could smell horseshit and piss and searched the trees till he spied the backside of one, maybe two painted ponies. He could see where their hooves had trampled the yellow-stained snow. Back in the trees was a lean-to and the fire and a single man draped in a buffalo robe. He watched carefully, letting the impressions grow into recognition, never thinking he understood the scene until he had worked over it. There was a rifle propped against a tree, near at hand. He took it for a buffalo gun, a Sharps 50 by the look, the big brother of his own but slow to reload. A sawbuck packsaddle and canvas packs sat at the back of the lean-to along with an old McClellan saddle, a string of steel traps tarnished with long use, a miner's pick and a shovel. He waited while the sun felt its way down the slant valley wall to the flats, and presently a second figure appeared from the direction of the horse line, buckling a belt round his pants, wearing a Union infantry cap and gimping on a bad left leg. Then he realized that the one in the buffalo robe wasn't a man but a woman.

He thought he had them figured now, but he waited just to be sure, and presently the smell of coffee drifted across the pond to where he lay. A horse nickered and tossed its head and tried to back out of its tether. The man hefted an axe and set up to split firewood. He rested the Sharps on a rock, threw away the first cap and fitted another over the nipple, then levelled the sights on the middle of the man's back as he raised the axe over his head, and shot him. The report rolled up the valley, then came back. He levered the chamber open before the man hit the ground, replaced the cartridge and cap, and took his second shot. The woman was already moving, rolling sideways over a log for cover, her hand reaching for the Big 50, but his bullet caught her in the head going down, sprouting a crimson mushroom where her ear had been.

Then he was running, reloading, cursing as the snow caught him and bowled him over. He held the rifle in the air even as he tumbled, rolled up on his feet and threw away another cap, replaced it and took aim in case someone was moving in the camp. But nothing moved. He went on at an easier pace, straight across the valley, crashing through the spring crust over and over, not stopping for the creek, nascent, engorged, descending like molten glass out of the pond over a beaver dam, but going straight in up to his chest with the Sharps overhead, fighting the current and feeling with his feet for holes or rocks, sinking into the cold gravel bottom. Stop and die, he thought. He cut for the treeline away from the camp and circled to come at it from beyond the tethered horses, still anxious he might have missed something. There were three Indian ponies, short-legged pintos with big heads, thick necks and scraggly manes, unshod but their hooves had been well trimmed.

He pushed cautiously into the campsite. The Big 50 still leaned against the tree. The woman breathed with a liquid rasp, her face swollen grey-blue, a plume of pinkish brain matter caught in her black hair. She was Snake by her tattoos, the ones they called Diggers for their primitive ways, built like a tugboat and tall for a woman. Her squaw-man was dead with a curiously bloodless hole going into his spine and a bigger hole coming out the front with the entrails bursting through and bits of bone. His forage cap was gone. The dead man was going to grey like himself, but with the added pathos of a bald spot like a monk's tonsure. He pulled the dead man's boot off, rolled up his trouser leg and found the scar where a Minié ball or a sliver of shrapnel had swept off most of the calf muscle. It was hard to say which side he had fought on. The forage cap didn't mean anything. The people coming west were mostly Southerners like himself. Both man and woman had their eyes open, but what they saw was in another world altogether.

He snapped up the Big 50 and the saddles and tack and quickly harnessed the horses, one for packing, two for riding, but one without a saddle. There was coffee, sugar, salt, flour, biscuits, salt beef and pemmican in the pack, also a cask of black powder, lead pigs, a bullet mould, wadding, pliers, a skinning knife and a wooden box containing nitric acid and aqua regia for testing gold. He rolled up the squaw's buffalo robe with another he found in the lean-to and lashed them both onto the mule pack with hide thongs. He hung the traps from the crossbuck, then coursed back and forth through the woods behind the campsite like a dog hunting a scent until he found the bale of furs—black bear, grey wolf and bobcat—hidden in a shallow overhang. He dragged the bodies under the lean-to then collapsed the frame over them, kicked out the fire. He believed the woman was still breathing when he left her, which he could scarcely credit, injured as she was, except that he knew when his time came it would be just as slow and difficult. He mounted and rode out, leading the pack horse and spare on a string, letting the horse pick its way along the flooded creek till he spied a likely ford and crossed, then clambered up past the elk bones. By the sun, it was just after noon.

In the Eyes of Another Man You See the Enemy

He incinerated the hut and the remains of the pole barn ere they departed and threw what bones he could find into the conflagration. Then they rode hard to the mouth of the valley into the high desert between the Lemhi Mountains and the Lost River Range where the Pashimeroi trickled like a green snake in the summer, the almost treeless mountain slopes on either hand covered in scree and dust-blown snow, looking like the mountains of the moon. At the river they reined north toward Leesburg and the Bitterroots. There was no track nor sign of travellers and after the third day when the thaw continued they slackened their pace to preserve the horses. But then, at the confluence of the Salmon, where they joined an old prospecting trail, they met a party of Bannocks, relatives of the Snakes, three men and a woman skinning a pronghorn buck, evidently joyful at their luck. They had but three sorry horses between them, bows and lances and a single muzzleloader; one was spitting blood. The men stood back suspiciously from their kill, notching arrows, and the woman stepped forward haranguing the strangers. She wore a black wool white-woman's skirt hiked up to her breasts and a cavalry trooper's jacket with the buttons and insignia removed, those lank breasts bare with nipples like walnuts.

They gave the Indians a wide berth, circling away from the arrows and then kicking up to a trot when they were into the trail again, quickly out of sight through the trees, the river gurgling over gravel drifts at the left. They kept on for a half mile, then he pulled up, dismounted, loaded the Big 50 and the Sharps, handed Good Luck the reins and said, "Ride on. Quick." Then he added, "But come back ere nightfall." And went to cover in a blowdown uphill from the river whence he could still see the trail. After an hour the Indians came on horseback, the woman riding double. They came silently, walking their horses, figuring to catch their prey when they camped. He let them ride so close there was no call for marksmanship and blew the shoulder off the first man with the Big 50, causing the woman some injury to her face, which appeared briefly as she fell from the horse, drabbled with gore like butchered meat, then dropped the second man with the Sharps. The third man had time to swing his mount, desperately thumping its scrawny flank with his bow, and dash down the trail. But he cleared the Sharps, loaded and fitted the percussion cap, aimed and shot the horse, severing one of the hind legs clean at the radius. Then he walked past the first set of bodies, still alive but moribund, reloading as he went, and killed the fallen rider where he fought to free his legs from under the struggling horse. He finished the others with his butcher knife, then dragged their bodies to the bank and heaved them into shallows. He caught their horses, retrieved the Big 50, and left the dying horse for varmints.

Why do they come after me? he thought. Why does the world insist? he thought. He lived in a slaughterous universe under a doleful sign of dream from which he did not wish to awaken, for that seemed like death to him. You stop and you die, he thought. He met the girl coming back to find him, which was a surprise as he expected betrayal at every turn. He followed her glance and noticed for the first time the hematitic stains on his hands, his arms and spattered on his shirt, as though he had bathed in blood. She dismounted and shuffled to him without her sticks, taking his hands in turn, inspecting them with her fingers, palpating for wounds, then suddenly grazing his wrist with her hungry tongue, a gesture he could not interpret, though he felt it directly in his balls as if his body had rendered up a meaning he could not himself name. He found her muteness eloquent in ways he could not explain; she did not deceive him, veiling herself in words as people generally did until he just wanted to shoot them to make them shut up and be.

Upriver, the land was scabbed and scotched with abandoned hydraulic mining works, dammed creeks, banks and hillsides scoured of trees and water-blasted, with gullies and fans of silt destroying the graceful curves of the old channel.

He killed three Chinamen damming a creek to feed their water machines, leaving their bodies floating face down in the icy pond. In examining their campsite, he found bottles of whiskey. He opened one, tilted it back, swallowed half without stopping to breathe, neatly capped the bottle again and returned to looting. Presently he discovered buffalo-robe bedding in the Chinamen's tent and went to ground there taking the bottle, which, when he looked again, was empty. At nightfall the girl joined him, bringing another bottle, and they drank together, then slept or fell unconscious. In his sleep, he heard the dead Chinamen whispering together under the reservoir water, speaking of the country whence they had come, of women they had loved, of poems they had once memorized, and of regret at not being alive. He woke and stumbled outside to piss and pissed against a tree and tripped over a tent peg and roared around the camp naked and sweating and feeling as if he had fallen into a fire he was that warm. Around him the forest seemed to glow. Stars glowed. It seemed to him the days and nights had reversed their orders. The girl appeared at the tent flap, swaying uncertainly in her boots, in his wife's last dress. He kicked her back into the buffalo skins, and when she tried to rise, he slapped her down, and then slapped her once more to inspire affection. Then he fell upon her with an untidy passion, not actually entering her, for she was ignorant and unhelpful in that regard, and presently reached the end of his desire in an onanistic paroxysm of shakes, grunts and incontinent dribbles. In that moment of sweet black forgetfulness he somehow recalled a singsong ditty his mother had crooned. At least he thought it was his mother, having no other memory of her save for the voice and the words. *Oh, you shall be my nevermind / and I will be your doxy / and we shall dance the night away / ere the ill winds blow.*

They met a tinker driving a garishly tricked-up John Deere freight wagon drawn by four snow-white Spanish mules with tin bells on their collars and periwinkle-coloured tassels nodding above their heads. Coming from the goldfields, the tinker's cart was light in goods, bouncing high over the ruts, but pregnant with the implication of cash money. Afrighted at the sight of the two asymmetric strangers who, yes, seemed almost to glow with a nimbus of menace, the tinker pulled a dragoon revolver that needed two hands to sight and shoot, and even then, with his nerves and the mad kick of the gun, he was only able to wound one of the Indian horses and a mule. With his third bullet, he shredded his foot, after which he became resigned to his fate. He said, "I will give you my money, but I know you are going to kill me surely." The stranger said, "Every man goes some time. Now's yers." The tinker said, "You are God's Hand. My foot hurts somethin' fierce. Do it quick."

In Leesburg, he sold the ponies, horses, mules, furs, buffalo gun, and various tools and artifacts he had collected along the way to a blacksmith at a quarter of what they were worth, which immediately attracted suspicion and notoriety, not to mention the fact that the blacksmith recognized the white mules and wondered where the tinker had got to. He bought two fresh horses and a pack mule and saddles and tack for all three and stabled the animals at a livery. He bought new clothes for himself and Good Luck and a Henry repeating rifle to go with the Sharps and then a pound of yellow cheese, white onions, beef jerky and a bottle of whiskey and retired with the girl to a hotel, where he had a tub and hot water brought to the room. He lay in the tub sipping whiskey, peeling and slicing the onions and eating them like apple quarters between bites of cheese. He bade the girl scrub his back with a rag, but she left off after a pass or two and presently he felt her strange tongue at the back of his neck, then licking water off his earlobe. He tried to kiss her, but she squirmed away. He had a hard-on now and tried to make her grasp it. But she would not come near. He drank more whiskey, and as the water was growing cold, he rose, wet and sickly white except for the leathery tan of his hands and face, stepped dripping to the bed and took the quilt to dry himself. Then he threw the girl—boots, dress and all—into the tub and said, "Now it's yer turn. Wash yerself. You stink." She dragged off his wife's last dress and then the boots and the wooden feet and crouched shivering in the shallow grey water with her arms across her breasts. He slugged whiskey from the upended bottle and examined his pecker, flicking off pebbles of smegma beneath the foreskin, stood and pissed a long arc into the tub and laughed and said, "That'll warm ye up." But he saw that she was weeping and could not evade him or escape the tub without the purchase of her feet.

The complexity of the situation, the misfire of his drunken overtures, now self-seen as awkward, if not moronic, enraged him. His first impulse was to strike, but unwitting, the impulse transmuted to his limbs became something else. He lifted Good Luck roughly from the tainted water, wrapping her in the quilt, and fell to examining the scars of her stumps, which he rubbed dry with a sheet, disturbed by the innocence of her pudenda fully displayed for him in the act of mercy. The scars were angry, puckered, purple lines etched clumsily into the whiteness of her flesh. "Do they fret ye?" he asked. She shook her head. "Some blistered," he said. "I will find ye better boots." He tipped water from the boots and dried them and dried the carved feet, pulling the sheets from the bed and using them to sop up the water. Then he left the boots to air with the sheepskins hung on the back of a chair, rolled Good Luck in the quilt with a pillow under her head, and said to sleep. He blew out the lamps and sat in his new shirt in a captain's chair by the glass window with the Henry and a box of shiny brass cartridges, felt for the brass follower with his fingers, drew it up against the spring to the top of the barrel, twisted the magazine open, and counted a dozen cartridges into the tube. Then he twisted the magazine closed and eased the follower down to the last cartridge lest the snap of the new spring accidentally set off the primers.

He stirred ere dawn, convinced he was being watched through the glass window where he had carelessly slept. He remembered the blacksmith's fleer as he counted out the money. He remembered the bones emerging from the snow, the burned-out wagons, the desolate campsites, the litter of corpses along the road coming up, the accumulated calculus of carnage vexing toward him, low breathing and indistinguishable motions just beyond his senses. Stop and die, he thought, slipping out of the hotel the back way to strangle the blacksmith in his sooty bed above the forge and retrieve the horses and tack. Flames from the burning smithy illuminated their backs as they rode away, long black shadows preceding them, deforming in the ruts, pursued by the slobber and shriek of horses in their panic, the thunder of guns as men shot the trapped horses through the burning stable walls. He said to the girl riding out, "I don't believe y've ever seen a body kiss before." She shook her head. "What strange world were ye a-born in?" And then he said, "I kilt the horse-shoer because he was blabbing about us." And then after a silence, when they had left the last of the Leesburg townsite and diggings behind and had seen nobody but a nigger with a wooden yoke and two steaming buckets of night soil, he said, "I don't believe yer ever going to speak to me." She shook her head. "I don't take it personal," he said. She wore a black full skirt hiked up to get her legs across the saddle; her boots cut into her flesh just below the knee and her thighs were bare except for the lace-hemmed lavender pantalets in the morning twilight. She had a warm wool coat, a knitted cap and a scarf and seemed, on the whole, pleased with herself.

Epithalamium

The weather held. They travelled fast at first, heading east from Leesburg, taking the saddleback pass over the Beaverheads toward Bloody Dick Creek and the Wisdom River, mostly avoiding the common trails and mining settlements because he felt at a disadvantage in the midst of a crowd and did not think he was riding faster than his legend. He killed now and then but tried to be prudent and reasonable in his depredations. "Why are you a-killing me?" one asked. "Because I am the Hand of God," he said. "Bullshit." Blam. One man he let go when the Sharps hung fire three times in a row. "Speak well of me," he said. "I will. Thank 'ee." One man said, "God help you. Kill me, but save my wife and childers." "I can't do that," he said. "May we say a family prayer first?" asked the man. "A short one, I hain't got all day." Blam. Always following the spring freshets swelling the creeks in the dry valleys in the shadow of noble mountains. And everywhere they found derelict sluices, dams, ditches, flumes, tailing pools, abandoned cabins, all evidence of the gold rush where the placers had petered out. "Are ye a preacher?" he asked. "No." Blam. "What do you want a preacher for?" "To get hitched." "Haha. That's a good 'un. To the crip?" Blam.

He rode toward the smoke-heaving blast furnaces of Bannack with a short string of stolen horses packed with loot, gold dust in his pockets, leaving Good Luck in camp in a spring-flower coulee stippled with pines where they had chanced upon a hot-water pool, the boulders and moss beds round about littered with eagle feathers, stone arrow points, beads and bits of bone left by the Indians. Dandling her legs in the pool to ease her stumps, she seemed like a whole girl, half smiling and twitching as the bubbles erupting from crevices below tickled her scars. And he thought were she to speak, it would complete the illusion. But then he thought, She does not speak because she sees her life as a dream, a nightmare, which, if she speaks, will only turn real. In town he listened to stories about himself in saloons where brave men spoke loudly of Vigilance Committees and hangings, in the company of other brave men, voices sounding of brass. But they made him anxious, every hand turned against him, even if they didn't know it was him, and there were too many to shoot. He bought three steers of a Christian stockman starting a spread on the Grasshopper Creek to drive ahead as a disguise and made for the coulee with coffee, a ribbon for the girl and whiskey bottles clinking in his saddlebags. Then, hidden from the eyes of men, he threw himself naked into the springs, scorching his skin pink, breaking the surface with a shout. He uncorked the store whiskey from his packs and stretched on a moss bed with Good Luck as the sun went down. He helped her shed her boots and clothing and coaxed her into the water. She gasped and flung her footless legs around him, her ribs sliding inside her skin each time she breathed, her small breasts like upturned cups, jewelled with water drops, slippery against his chest. She burrowed against his neck and licked and sucked his skin. "I ain't a tit," he said, attempting to kiss her, but she would not. Then, with the heat of the spring water and the excitement of their parts rubbing together, he shot his load into the seething effervescence, cried out a cry of pathos and dismay, and seemed to fall into a black pit. Coming to himself, he heard the mother voice, the words. *Oh, you shall be my nevermind / and I will be your doxy / and we shall dance the night away / ere the ill winds blow.*

Then it was summer, rainless and arid, except high in the mountain ranges where snow yet clung in the sawtooth creases. They pushed their steers up the dusty stage road that ran from Fort Hall to the placer fields at Alder Gulch and Helena, lazily working their way north but watchful, driving the steers to the river to drink when they descried the thunderous clatter of the freight wagons drawing near. It was far too crowded, he thought. Up every creek, fork and gulch, he found the detritus of human occupation. At every stream bend, a Chinaman with a pan, dipping for gold. Furtive Indians hunted in the cottonwoods. On the four quarters, black smoke rose from the furnaces. Stages ground by like clockwork, stations for changing horses measured every fifteen miles. Teamsters thrashed their long trains up and down the roadstead, leaving a fine white dust to settle like mortuary lime. Painted signs nailed to posts marked the forks, made poetry of commerce. Dark Horse, Puzzler, Blue Wing, Polaris, Argenta, Hecla, Queen of the Hills, Pandora. Industrious avidity, he thought. Busy and inquisitive as rats, he thought. It wasn't that he was against the making of money, but he hewed to a desperate and higher calling, a dark path bequeathed him in the cornfield at Antietam, which rendered his character contemptuous.

He held to the high mountains on his left and presently veered away from the Wisdom River, following a tributary in a narrow, sere valley. Some distance off the trail and out of sight up a gulch that had barely been touched by placers, they discovered a cabin and pole barn and an acre cleared of everything but stumps and wildflowers, and beyond, among the sparse pines, beef cattle foraging. The owner and his wife politely took them in for the night. He shot them after dinner and stored the bodies in a convenient cold cellar made of rock slabs, chilled by a mountain spring that bubbled out of a crevice. He turned his steers loose amongst the others, and because he paid them no mind, they disappeared up or down the cold, splashy creek. Then untold days passed and he wished for that Plott hound of the prior winter, for there were bears about and he wanted to hunt. The girl unscrolled a buffalo robe and lay naked, save for boots, in the cleared field when the sun shone, turning dusky brown so her eyes smouldered and her bleached hair was like a white flame. He discovered a six-month-old newspaper from St. Louis in the cabin and read to her in bed by candlelight. Pronghorns concoursed in the cleared field in the twilight gloom ere dawn; he shot one when they needed it. A lonely prospector with a mule and a donkey, a twelve-month growth of yellow beard and no teeth to speak of stumbled upon the homestead one sunspill afternoon. He said, "That girl is like enough half Indian parading without drawers. I could do er. I could." And then he said, "No, I ain't a preacher, but I read the Good Book when I were a sprout and have took the pledge at camp meetin' to go teetotal when I am not drinking." Blam. His body went into the cold cellar with the others.

He rode to Butte to sell stolen horses. He did not like the open country there, the buffalo prairie and the dry gulches filled with abandoned placer equipment and the scattered settlement of mean log houses, slanted frame buildings leaning together, the skeletal remains of the silver smelter, and nary a place to conceal himself. In the saloon next to Hauswirth's Hotel on Main Street he heard how a Vigilance Committee at Last Chance Gulch had captured him twice but he had escaped both times by trickery or infernal magic. A Mormon bone collector hunting buffalo kills had spied him slaughtering a human corpse far north in the Flatheads. When he checked on the return trip, parts of the body had been chewed on. After asking nine people in that depressed and irreligious town for directions, he tracked down a placer miner name of Skloot who once had been a preacher, was an undertaker on the side and could also cure the toothache with a red-hot wire. Skloot had five children out of eighteen born and introduced a young wife Priscilla Skloot who was his second wife after the first succumbed in giving birth. "How far did yer say was yer camp?" asked Skloot. "About five mile. You'll be back ere nightfall." After they had ridden fifteen miles, Skloot said, "I know who ye are. I should have known from the start." Skloot was working on his portly successful look and his horse wore a bloom of frothy sweat. He had brought a Bible, a shotgun in a saddle holster and a half-dozen boiled eggs for his lunch. The stranger rode behind him now but sidled up to offer him a slug of store whiskey, which the preacher took willingly. He said, "My first drap in six years. I believe the occasion requires it."

They were both tight when their horses clambered up through the cleared field to the cabin, the keynotes of roast antelope, woodsmoke and some other noxious, unidentifiable odour drifting down to welcome them. Bees hummed in the wildflowers. Skloot tumbled from his horse dismounting and trembled upon his back with one foot caught in the stirrup. He said, "I have drunk with the Devil and now I will die and speak with Jesus on the same day. That must be the record." "Just get up and say the words," said the stranger, handing him the Bible. He opened another bottle and handed that over too. He carried the preacher's shotgun in the crook of his elbow. Good Luck leaned against him, her hands braced on her sticks, her face blank and hairless, her hairless eyelids lizard-like, eyes like blue stones, her pox scars like craters, her general air uncanny. That much had not changed since he first clapped eyes on her. "Is she a squaw?" asked Skloot. "What's wrong with her?" "Many have died for asking," said the stranger. "I'm sure they have," said Skloot, sucking on the whiskey and gradually working his way upright with the aid of the stirrup and saddle straps. "Under the circumstances," he said, "I believe the abbreviated version of the order of service will suffice. Do you two want to get married?" "She can't talk," said the stranger. "Good enough," said Skloot. "I now pronounce you man and wife, all square and legal, and may God help me for what I have just done." The stranger squeezed the girl's hand. That was all. He said, "Come with me. I want ter show ye something." He led the preacher along the faint convexity in the pine needles to the cold cellar where the stone entry buzzed with bluebottles. Skloot's eyes watered from the stench. The girl followed on, swinging upon her sticks, her hair a flame like the head of a torch. The light was lingering toward dusk. The stranger stood by as Skloot stooped to peer inside where a dozen or more swollen green bodies lay stacked like cordwood, in a state of putrefaction so horrific that they seemed to be melting, their juices funnelling together and emerging into a pool amongst the ferns and quartz boulders just outside the hellish door. Hundreds of flies lined the sides, lapping and rubbing their feet in the sludge like holy pilgrims. Skloot reeled away, but not able to take his eyes off those carbonizing corpses, their infernal hutch, he slipped, landing smartly on his portly ass, scrambling backwards, still staring. Then he wrenched up his shirt-tails and threw them over his face, gasped and cried out, "Dear Lord, please shoot me now. Get it over with. Stop this persecution. I cannot bear the waiting. I wish to God I had not seen that." "I ain't going ter shoot ye," said the stranger. "I just wanted to show ye. Ye could have slept with them tonight, but ye did me a good turn. It's nigh dusk. Ye should mount and kick up for home ere my resolution falters." And then he added, "Ye will send a committee back for me, I know. I expect it. But they shall not find me. And this night will be in yer heart forever."

1910, Sellwood, Oregon

They lived now in a two-storey clapboard house on Umatilla Street within sight of the Willamette River, rented two rooms on the second floor to lodgers, kept a garden, laying hens and a cow, and were noted for their exceptional aloofness. The old man worked at the M & H Foundry on 13th Street that manufactured parts for the Sellwood Car House and other railroad concerns in Portland but had suffered a stroke some time before and was only kept on as a sweeper out of charity and fear. He could no longer speak except in garbled syllables, the left side of his face drooped, his eye leaked, and evenings he sat on the porch in a wicker rocker with his hands on his knees, his fingers picking at the fabric of his trousers, his eyes bearing outward at some inscrutable distance, seeing what no one else could see. Only the new motor cars puttering by in the street seemed to excite in him a special admiration; Sundays he rode the ferry to Portland to look at the electric street lights whose fierce and mysterious flame fascinated him, though he could never explain why. And yet there was still something furious and wilful in his look that gave men pause.

Good Luck always sat inside at the window where she could watch him, her face hidden by the chintz curtains, reading the newspaper with spectacles by an oil lamp or knitting or mending for the lodgers, for which she charged extra. She wore starched shirtwaists with pearl buttons up to her throat and black skirts and walked with the aid of two vine-twisted mahogany canes with elk-antler handles. The canes and the boots she wore—handmade reinforced Spanish calf-leather boots that laced up to her knees—were the only luxuries in the otherwise spare and spartan house. The boarders were Miss Adeline Frick, a schoolteacher, and Francis Ward, a law clerk, both of whom were anxious to move on for reasons they could not specify aside from the prevalence of bad dreams in that house, the cold, silent and remote atmosphere, and the aura of threat which seemed to clash with the manifest fragility of their hosts.

One evening late in the summer, a stranger knocked. Dinner was on the stove, the boarders were not yet in for the night. The stranger showed her a badge, said he was a policeman from Helena, Montana, that he wanted to speak to them of an old case about which they might have information. He was wearing a suit and a fedora with the brim neatly snapped down at the front. He carried a carpet bag, which he left on the porch by the rocker. He was robust but limped, dragged a chair to the dining table but sat awkwardly, one leg unable to bend at the knee, and dealt out newspaper clippings like a deck of cards, yellowed clippings, curled like leaves, from Arco, Leesburg, Bannack, Dillon, Butte, Virginia City, Coeur d'Alene and Spokane, dating back as far as the 1870s. The clippings were full of sensational stories: a disappearance here, charred bones discovered there, mutilated corpses, mining camp massacres, isolated homes burned, dismemberments, cannibal rites and ghastly, inhuman practices. The old man crouched at the head of the table, his puttied face sad as a clown's, gnarled, scarred hands on his knees, apparently oblivious or worse, not present at all, but seething inwardly, on the half-cock with no one able to pull the trigger. In fact, he heard everything. He thought, You stop and you die. But this was the inner voice of a will that had lost the power of action without great forethought and deliberate steps. He was thinking how best to rise from his seat and repair to the cellar, where he kept his guns. His eyes rose to meet Good Luck's gaze, which remained opaque, her epalpebrate eyes sinister, the pox scars splashed across her face like stars. Once he had spelled them out with a book in the candlelight. Alwaid, Etamin and Thuban.

The policeman was maybe thirty but youthful, excited by knowledge, not caring so much for justice or punishment but wanting to be the one who put the puzzle together. In Spokane in 1874, he said, a derelict nigger, who confessed to a dozen acts of arson and mayhem, had been charged, convicted and hanged before a Baptist minister from Butte came forward with a tale that seemed to exonerate him. The preacher had met a vagrant couple, the girl crippled in both legs, the two of them giving off an appalling and horrific odour of otherworldly malevolence, a whiff of the demonic, as though they had ridden together from out of the Land of the Dead, where, as he thought, they had no doubt returned. The stranger had conversed with the preacher; the girl had no words, it seemed. The stranger gave the preacher a parable, grisly enough to scare him half to death, into a haunted and impeccable silence. The preacher's exact words were, "He drug me to the Gate of Hell and let me look inside."

The young policeman's notebooks tumbled out of his pockets onto the table, the pages dense with pencilled interviews, transcribed reports, rumours, legends, theories. He had uncovered numerous sightings of this identical couple, a man with a crippled girl, from Arco up to the Salmon River and thence to the old post road connecting the Oregon Trail to the goldfields of Montana; from Butte, where the preacher had met them, to the Boise gold diggings; and on into Washington, chance sightings mostly, fleeting and from afar, the couple caught drifting just at the world's periphery, but the two of them together so peculiar, enigmatic and uncanny that they remained fixed in memory long after the mundane had faded. It was as if they existed within the order of dream, more real than real, though the trail they left was clear and palpable enough. He had himself examined boxes of bones. And yet no one knew them.

The policeman watched Good Luck press herself up from the table, gather her sticks and limp to the kitchen to tend the dinner. His cheek twitched in a half smile of barely repressed triumph. The old man grunted and signalled for a notebook and pencil. His hand trembled as he carved the letters on the ruled page. "Did ye bring a gun?" he wrote. The policeman unlapped the tail of his coat to show his holster and the pistol tucked inside. The old man strained to see. "It's a Colt, military issue," said the policeman. "Forty-five-caliber semi-automatic, loaded with hollow points, seven in the clip." The old man grunted again, satisfied. "How did you get yer wound?" he wrote. "The Battle of the Malalag River, 1905. We were clearing the Cotabato Valley. A Moro sniper blew up my knee. How did you know?" The old man couldn't answer. He wanted to talk about the cornfield when the Texians marched in to plug a gap in the line with their bodies and succeeded, not some skirmish with ill-armed savages in the god-fuck Philippines. Good Luck pushed a serving trolley through the kitchen doorway with a coffee pot and cups and dinner plates, cutlery and a water jug. The old man hunched over the notebook, licked his lips and wrote again, hesitating over the letters. "What do ye intend with us?" The policeman was at the old man's elbow now, craning his neck to read the words, his fingers reaching to tilt the page to the light. Good Luck set a cup at his place, but he took no notice. Then she snatched the butcher knife and plunged it into his throat, searching for the artery, a freshet of spermy red blood bubbling out. The policeman gasped, but the old man had an iron grip on his wrists, and for a fatal moment he could not but gaze unapprehending at the hand that gripped the knife and the knife handle and the current of blood staining Good Luck's shirt sleeve. And then the light began to ebb like water going out, he felt unutterably defeated by things, he had grasped the secret but in the instant of his dying it escaped him, in the instant of his death he guiltily remembered spying on his mother naked before the washstand mirror, in the instant of his dying he was embarrassed.

The old man dragged the policeman's body into the pantry, not bothering about the incarnadine smear of blood he painted across floorboards. Good Luck poured coffee, and he field-stripped the pistol while they waited on the return of the boarders. He released the magazine and pulled back the slide to check the chamber, then he depressed the take-down plug under the barrel opening and pushed out the slide lock. He cocked the hammer with his thumb and pulled the slide back and off the receiver. Then he put it back together, chambered a round and drank his coffee. He killed Francis Ward and Miss Adeline Frick when they came like lambs through the front door. He laid their bodies side by side under the dining table, then collected the newspaper clippings and notebooks and burned them in the firebox of the cookstove. He brought the carpet bag inside and turned it upside down, searching for more paper evidence, but found none except an envelope with five postcards of naked women, which he also consigned to the fire.

Now he was exhausted and confused. His mind ran away from his body the way it had when he was alone and starving to death under the sheepskins that long-ago winter. He wanted a horse, he thought. Two horses, a mule, tack and grub. But where would they ride? He was a soul inside a corpse, hard clay, difficult to convince of the necessity of action, all used up in the events of the last hour. He wasn't defeated, he told himself, only indignant at the puny nature of flesh, this squalid frame for the implacable hunger that dwelt inside and through which he was connected to every other living thing. The mother voice sang in his head. *Oh, you shall be my nevermind / and I will be your doxy.* He recalled a blue girl on a glistening hill. He examined Good Luck's face for a sign but found there only the same old terrible resoluteness of spirit, wordless and endless. He wanted to speak, but speech failed. How alike they had become in the expanse of time.

He tucked the Colt inside his waistband then staggered into the kitchen pantry, retrieved their stocks of kerosene and coal oil, and doused the floor. He lifted the chimney off the lamp at the dining table, turned up the wick and threw the lamp. We are purified in the fire, he thought. Redeemed from seethe and scorn, he thought, and preserved from the corruption of memory. With the hot tongues of flame licking up the walls and smoke rippling across the ceiling, they supported each other to the ground-floor room where they slept, leaving the door ajar—nothing to keep out, he thought, nothing to fear. They lay together on the counterpane. He clutched the pistol in his right hand. He thought he would not need it. In the strange light, her lips seemed to contort as though she laboured under a compulsion to speak, but he knew that she would not. *And we shall dance the night away / ere the ill winds blow.*

Crown of Thorns

When Tobin was eight, he fell in love with his babysitter Aganetha, the awkward one with the large, damp eyes, floppy, uncontrollable bosoms and a soot-coloured hairwing she kept pulled down over her face to hide her acne. One night, waking up to pee, Tobin spied Aganetha and his father embracing in the rose arbour at the back gate. Aganetha's sweatshirt was rucked up at her throat, her bra askew, one breast dislodged and bright as a second moon. The scene was enveloped in silence, lit by a real moon hanging over the garden like a Japanese lantern or a breast. Dormant, dither, delft, dreadful, death and dalliance—*d*-words from his book droned through Tobin's head. Seeing the breast flattened against his father's hand, Aganetha's pale flesh bulging like putty between the rough, muscular fingers, Tobin thought, She must be cold. Then his mother was standing just behind him, in his bedroom by the back window, her fingernails chill talons digging into his shoulder. He thought, he made a connection, never to be obliterated from memory: My mother's hand on my shoulder is just like my father's hand on Aganetha's breast. He wet his pyjamas right down to the floor.

Aganetha disappeared from Tobin's life. He thought of her as a kite, but the string had snapped and she was drifting away from him. His parents never mentioned her. He thought, She is the only person I ever loved. She is my beginning and my end. His mother, if anything, seemed warmer, more attentive, toward his father, but in an anxious, frenzied, hysterical manner that he later described to his therapist as a theatre of martyrdom. See, she seemed to say, I am the perfect one for you because I will bear anything, tolerate every betrayal and vice. To Tobin, his father seemed ineffably distant, cruel, cold, powerful and perverse. Both his parents were so involved in their private drama that they had no emotion to spare for Tobin. He thought, he told the therapist, he was having a happy childhood.

With Aganetha gone, life seemed like a dream to Tobin. He did not know why anything occurred or what was real. He began to wet the bed. It just happened, he explained to his mother. Someone else was controlling his bodily functions. Erections were inexplicable and usually accompanied some act of cruelty. He got erections when he threw rocks at the neighbour's puppy Squiggles. He got erections when he found his mother weeping in the rose arbour. He got erections every time he passed through the rose arbour. One day he threw himself against the rose arbour, impaling himself on the thorns, an image of the Jesus he had seen in his children's Bible. When the blood came, he had an erection. He remembered Aganetha's breast in his father's hand and had his first orgasm.

He was suddenly twelve and enrolled in a special school. He couldn't understand why he was there. He told the school counsellor about his love for Aganetha, whom he assumed was dead, murdered, yes, by his father, with the help of his mother. He knew where she was buried.

"This explains why you keep digging up the rose arbour," said the therapist, reading from his notes.

"I don't know why I dig there," said Tobin. "I am controlled by outside forces, my mother and father, I think. They have a remote control transmitter and there is a chip embedded in my skull. When I dig in the back garden, I feel peaceful."

"Why do you stick pencils in your penis?" asked the therapist.

"That's easy," said Tobin. Then he fell silent. Then he said, "There is a button. If they press that button, my head will explode and I'll be dead."

"Do you think your parents love you?" asked the therapist.

"Absolutely," said Tobin.

*

After the special school, there was an away school, then the incident with the school nurse's kitten, the fires, another school, the Internet pornography ring featuring first- and second-graders in the school washroom, shoplifting, juvenile detention. In group therapy at the Cedar Vale Centre, Tobin met a depressed girl named Rose who was addicted to several drug groups and had dabbled in prostitution. She was overweight, her breasts swung like giant pods beneath her sweatshirt, she had lank black hair and a crucifix tattooed on her forehead. She taught Tobin to hold his breath till he fainted. Nights, Tobin dreamed he saw his father kissing Rose in the rose arbour, kneading her chubby breasts with his clawlike fingers. He showed Rose a photograph of his father. She said she might have known him, or someone just like him, a double.

Tobin said, "I can hold my breath till I'm dead."

"Have you ever been kissed?" asked Rose. When he did not answer, she asked, "Have you ever made love?"

At which point Tobin fainted.

He bought a crown of thorns plant with his pocket money and kept it by his bedside. He changed therapy groups and avoided Rose, even when she wept and threatened to kill herself. His new therapist asked him what he made of the fact that his family name was Thorn. Tobin held his breath until he passed out. Seeing himself in the men's room mirror, in the ghastly glow of the strip lights, he realized he was beginning to look like his father. They had the same sinister leer, the same feminine belly, the same hermaphrodite penis. This realization gave him an erection. He felt suddenly powerful. He felt an overpowering urge to find Rose or to dig a hole. But Rose had mysteriously left Cedar Vale. No one could explain it, but he took it as a sign of love.

Years seemed to pass. Tobin (Thorn), along with his crown of thorns plant, moved back with his parents. The house had an antiseptic air, something like a barracks or a prison, much like Cedar Vale Centre. His mother and father rarely spoke to Tobin, or anyone else for that matter. They locked him in his room at night. Their lives seemed shrouded in a dense, greasy fog. They moved awkwardly around the house in synchronized patterns like automata. They wore matching cardigan sweaters with deep pockets. At night he could hear them weeping. The backyard was pocked with unfilled holes, the rose arbour upended, the roses dead, their arched stems prickly in the moonlight like the backs of prehistoric monsters. He looked for jobs involving excavation. He found himself attracted to backhoes and barbed wire. He wore a cardigan sweater with deep pockets. He thought how everything repeated in his life, beginning with the moment when he fell in love with Aganetha. There were remnants of yellow plastic police tape in the backyard. When he came home, there had been a pile of letters in an unknown handwriting. He dared not open them, but he fondled them and got erections. After he got an erection, he would wet the bed. His erections were signs that a higher power was controlling him. The mysterious envelopes prompted him to write letters to the newspapers accusing the staff of Cedar Vale Centre of murdering Rose and concealing her body on the grounds. He also mentioned the alarming disappearance of a girl named Aganetha some years before. He fell in love with the music of Kurt Cobain. When the police came, he remembered the psychologist from before.

She said, "You know your parents say there never was a babysitter named Aganetha."

Tobin (Thorn) said, "Without Aganetha I am nothing."

At the cemetery where he found work, Tobin met a woman named Dolores. She was typical of the women to whom he found himself attracted—melancholy, shy, sexually demanding, lonely, and possessed of large breasts. She lay down beside a headstone (a rose engraved in granite) and invited him to have sex with her.

After he fainted, she said, "Are you a virgin?"

He said, "Every woman I have loved has been murdered."

"Was that before or after you had sex?" she asked.

"Before," he said.

Tobin felt himself getting woozy again, talking so intimately with those large breasts, which, now that he thought of it, reminded him of his mother. Once, he had seen his mother naked on her bed, her breasts slung to the side; like boat bumpers, he thought.

"Then you're a virgin," said Dolores. "How old are you?"

"Forty-two," he said.

"You've wet your pants," she said.

*

Everything reminded Tobin of everything else, as if the world were made up of signs and omens that only referred to other signs and omens. He understood that his life was ruled by a principle of recursion. It occurred to him that he might be nothing but a robot with a short circuit, that consciousness was a flaw that only caused anguish, anxiety and alienation. He filled his room with thorny houseplants—barrel cacti, firethorn, Argentine mesquite, stinging nettle, Russian thistle, acacia, goat's thorn—so that he could sleep safely at night, though twice he tripped and impaled himself inadvertently. His shrieks went unanswered. His body was a star map of scars and punctures. He remained terrified of his father, a man now broken in health and feeble from the strain of defending himself against his son's accusations. His father had moved into an extended care facility, but Tobin's mother refused to tell him the address.

"Haven't you done enough?" she said.

There had been a restraining order, at least once. Every day, when he left for work, he would knock on his mother's door, give her a peck on the cheek, and say, "I love you, Mom." Each time, she seemed to shrink from him, shuddering, growing into herself, frail and sickly.

He tried to have his name legally changed from Thorn to Pillow. He went around introducing himself as Martin Pillow even though everyone knew him as Tobin Thorn. The house had fallen into ruin. Tobin sometimes borrowed the backhoe from the cemetery. He had undercut the foundation and knocked over the summer kitchen. One day Tobin's mother, no doubt consumed with jealousy over his hard-won success and happiness, packed an overnight bag and ran away with a man named Reggie Wemyss whom she had met when he came to the door selling vinyl replacement windows. She wrote in soap on the bathroom mirror: *Free At Last!* She did not leave a forwarding address. Tobin's new girl had roses tattooed on her breasts, a crown of thorns on her back, and a skein of barbed wire inked around her neck.

"Nobody can touch me," she said.

"No need to explain," he said.

They had met during grief therapy. She idolized Kurt Cobain. She called Tobin Martin Pillow because that was how he introduced himself. She was overweight, with large, unmanageable breasts, lank black hair turning to grey. She seemed alarmingly familiar, like every other woman in his life, but none the worse for having spent the last thirty years underground in the backyard.

"I thought you were dead," said Tobin. "Murdered."

"I don't know what you're talking about," she said. "But you've got me intrigued."

The new girl reminded Tobin of a kite come to earth, crumpled, broken, but still buffeted by the winds of desire. She showed him her paint-by-numbers Colonial America collection. She wore a cardigan sweater with deep pockets. She set the alarm clock at night and made him get up to pee. She taught him to play cribbage. They did jigsaw puzzles together. He took evening classes in power shovels and earth movers. They started a retirement account at the local credit union, bought a time-share in Boca Raton and joined the End Times Church of Christ the Reanimate, run out of a Trim-n-Buff nail salon in the mall. In his spare time Tobin began to write a self-help guide for abused children. Nights, he dreamed of being buried alive and premature ejaculation. Tobin told his therapist that his life was shadowed by forgotten things.

"Like what?" asked the therapist.

"I've forgotten," said Tobin.

He said he believed his parents had undergone plastic surgery and moved into the house next door under the names Mr. and Mrs. Kirpal Singh, an insidious couple with a small child named Parvati. Their cats came into his yard and did their business in the excavations. He had notified the police on several occasions. He and his new girl moved around the house in synchronized patterns like automata. At night he could hear her weeping behind locked doors. Aside from the violent rages, intermittent catatonia, nightmares, sleepwalking, chronic priapism, nervous hair-pulling, delusions of grandeur, deathly boredom, spiritual emptiness and sleep apnea, he felt that life had never been better.

One day, Tobin spotted Aganetha in the street. It was as though he had entered the Land of the Dead. There were gods everywhere. All of life had been a promise. His iguana brain rejoiced in the sunlight. Her hair was the colour of slate. She had breasts like liquid fuel rockets. He remembered first love. She was his beginning and his end. He remembered hope. He remembered her nervous whisper, her habit of eating her hair when she was thinking. He remembered she could make quarters dance on her knuckles and disappear. Then he noticed the tall silver-haired gent guiding her toward a black SUV, and the two cherubic teenagers, a boy and a girl, both resembling their parents. They were like visitors from another planet. His ardent heart heaved with adoration, yearning, jealousy, humiliation and rage. "What about me?" he screamed, heaving a rock like a prayer. Then he threw another rock. Who are those people? he thought. The rock clanged off the SUV. Stern faces leafed toward him like pages in a book. The boy nodded omnisciently. The silver-haired gent aimed an elegant pointer finger at the tip of a long arm. They possessed all the qualities Tobin lacked—grace, affection, sang froid, maturity and wisdom. For all Tobin knew, pure ichor ran in their veins. Aganetha gave him an ominous wave, almost as if she regretted it. If she is real, he thought, what of my dreams? my life? He held his breath. He willed himself not to breathe.

The wind suddenly picked up. A dust devil swirled toward him, whipping street grit into his eyes, stinging his cheeks like nettles. Aganetha kept waving like a railway signal, the rhythmic motion of her hand uncanny and mesmerizing. Her face was molten wax. Her eyes were like pits. Tobin felt the wind lifting him, felt himself the centre of storm. She mouthed the words, *I'm sorry.* The roar of the wind was terrific. He had to shut his eyes. His lungs were full of sand. His heart ached. The sound of the wind was like an explosion.

He remembered everything — his father's hand on a breast, the rose arbour, his mother's hot breath on his cheek, the absolute density of the moment from which all meaning emanated. There was always someone coming between you and the thing you love, he thought. Aganetha reminded him of a kite. He was holding the reel, but the line had broken. The kite was almost out of sight. All he had was the reel and a piece of broken string.

Light Trending to Dark

The trouble began when Lily, a girl I had been seeing, phoned the house one night last summer and spoke to my wife. They talked for an hour, talked like old friends. I was in and out of the sewing room, caught snatches of conversation and brittle laughter, suspected nothing. Then my wife—her name is Ellen—said would I watch the children for half an hour? She had to meet someone for coffee. She never met anyone for coffee, especially not in the evening.

"Who?" I asked.

"No one you know," she said, a little stiff, not to be argued with. She gets this way sometimes. She'd had a drink or two earlier.

"No problem," I said.

As soon as she left, the phone rang again. It was Lily. "I just talked to your wife, Ricardo. She's coming over to see me."

"Are you crazy?" I said. "And my name's not Ricardo."

"You blew it," she said. "You said you were leaving her. You said it's a dead marriage."

"You're killing me," I said.

"I'm killing you?" she said. "You think it feels good to find out the man you love has been lying to you all along? She says it's the first she's heard. She says you have a happy, stable marriage and three daughters under the age of eight. She's studying to be a Jungian therapist—you said she stayed home with the kids and sewed party dresses all day."

"I never told you that," I said.

"Here's a test," she said. "Did you have sex with your wife last night?" I tried to think. "Did you? You told me sex ended a year ago. You have to think about it?"

I groaned. "Listen, Lily," I said, "you can't talk to her any more. You'll break her heart. I was going to let her down easy."

"I think she's here," said Lily. "She thought it was kind of funny when I told her we meet up for quickies when you walk the dog."

"You'll ruin everything," I said.

"Yeah, yeah, yeah," she said. "I'll send her back in an hour."

I poured myself an Old Crow on the rocks and sat on the toilet seat while the girls splashed happily in the tub. They were wild, sensing something violent and threatening in the atmosphere. Before I knew it, they were taking turns sliding headfirst down the back of the tub, sending waves of soapy water whooshing onto the bathroom floor. Sophie knocked her forehead on the spout and started to bleed. Forehead wounds are bleeders, always look worse than they are. She bled into the tub, where the blood swirled and coiled like red smoke, then turned cloudy and dark, more blood than I'd ever seen before. I clamped a washcloth over the wound, but the blood seeped through and dripped down her nose. The two littler girls started to shriek in panic. I shouted at them to get in their PJs. They tracked blood down the hallway to their room. I put Sophie's hand on the washcloth and went to pour myself another bourbon.

In the kitchen, I rinsed the empty ice cube tray and refilled it, listening to my hysterical children in the background. The dog was barking at some phantom out the sliding door at the back. I could see the driveway. Ellen had taken the Saab. That sucker was about to be repossessed, I thought. Enjoy it while you can. I drank my drink and shouted at the girls to get their bathrobes on. We were going to take Sophie to the Emergency Room. I poured another drink.

Isobel came into the kitchen with her hamster cage in her arms. She said, "I think Pinky is dead." Her face was ashen, her tone grim. Sophie sobbed somewhere in the depths of the house.

I gulped back the drink and pushed past Isobel to the bathroom. I was a little drunk. I began to wonder if there were arteries in the forehead. Sophie was rinsing the washcloth in the sink while fresh blood bubbled out of her brow. I wrapped her in a towel and picked her up, carried her to the bedroom, and started putting her in underpants and PJs. Isobel came in after us, looking tragic.

The phone rang. It was Ellen.

"We have a situation here," I said.

"You rat," she said. "You utter shit."

"Pinky died," I said. "Maybe it's not the best time to talk this over."

"I'm at Lily's apartment," she said. "How old is this girl?"

"I don't know," I said. "Maybe twenty-five, twenty-six."

"She's twenty-*one*," said my wife. "I can't believe you did this." Her voice contained a note of malicious glee. Like many of us, my wife felt obscurely persecuted most of the time. No doubt it was a relief to find her paranoid fancies confirmed.

"Listen," I said, "I really think I should—Jesus, can you bleed to death from the forehead?"

"The hamster is bleeding to death?" she asked.

"No," I said. "Sophie hit her head in the tub. It's pretty bad. I'm taking her to the ER."

"Oh, Christ," she said. "Wait there for me."

"No, I'll meet you," I said. "I think I'd better get a move on."

I changed Sophie out of her bloody pyjamas and put fresh ones on and wrapped a towel around her head as tight as I could. Isobel stood there peering gravely down at her hamster. It looked as if it might just be sleeping soundly. "Did you poke it?" I asked. "Shake the cage a little." I watched the hamster bounce up and down in a cloud of wood shavings. It was sleeping very soundly.

"Honey," I said, "we have a situation here with Sophie that takes priority." Her eyes began to swim.

I went into the kitchen to pour myself another drink. I thought about Lily, whom I had met at the public library during Sophie's violin lesson. I generally dropped Sophie at her violin teacher's apartment after school those days and waited at the library, leafing through magazines and a book on how things work I had found in the Juvenile Non-Fiction section. It made me feel good to look at the pictures and captions and begin to understand something of MP3 players, tablet computers and liquid fuel rockets. One of the problems with life these days is the way technology has gotten away from us. Everything is a black box with an on/off switch. We can't fix a thing once it's broken any more. It really helped to see pictures of the insides of ordinary household items, to see their mysterious inner workings.

I trusted Sophie to walk the three blocks from her violin teacher's place, but one day she walked in with this strange girl —swarthy complexion, thick, dark eyebrows, nervous eyes, intelligence written all over her, along with adventurousness and low self-esteem. Sophie led her to me, and we started to talk while my daughter played math challenges on the computer. We had a lot in common: we both liked to talk about ourselves and we were both polite listeners. She started meeting me when I walked the dog at night. One thing led to another. She said she loved me. I didn't believe her and I didn't think she believed herself. We were both playing a little game. I said I loved her. Then I would come home and tell my girls I loved them and kiss Ellen good night and tell her I loved her. I was full of love.

Straggling through the garage door to the Subaru, we somehow let the dog out. This was bad. She was a German shepherd, frightened people. Also, when she got away she'd run down Pulver to number 81, where there was a chow permanently chained in the breezeway. I didn't know what my dog and the chow had in common, but that was where my dog went. When she finally came home, she generally vomited once or twice on the carpets. I didn't know what she ate at the chow's house. Sometimes I wondered if the chow's owners were trying to poison my dog. I kept thinking I'd go over there one night and find out what my dog's secret life really consisted of. Isobel had the hamster cage. Katie was sniffling, somewhat catatonic with emotional overload and sleep deprivation (it was ten minutes past her bedtime). Sophie's bleeding was beginning to ebb; possibly she'd lost all the blood there was to lose. The dog made me unreasonably angry. I thought, I'll kill the dog.

I seatbelted the girls and nestled my drink in the cup tray between the seats, blasted out of the garage like a Saturn rocket and swung onto the street. The house was ablaze with lights. There was a steady tick in the engine, the sound of machine deterioration, the approach of entropy. I couldn't afford to fix it. When I complained, Ellen said I didn't have a right. I had quit my steady job with the big stable company to chip in with a friend who owned a software start-up. He'd invented a surefire cellphone app that was going to make us rich. I spent four days a week in the air, flying home on weekends, flying high, Ellen said. We built the house. I bought the Saab, a lap pool, widescreen TVs, every gadget going. Ellen became a soccer mom (studying to be a Jungian therapist). Now the house was under water, I had my CV posted on the Internet, and I had plenty of spare time. I couldn't get over any of this. You think you know how things work, that you have some control, then you realize you're on a ride—you can't see the road and you're not sure there's a driver. The kind of world we're in makes us all gamblers and losers. You spend your life trying to get a handle on things, then you die, or worse, you die in some long, painful and humiliating manner. Maybe I was scared before this and didn't know it. But now I knew it. I looked down the road and I felt sick.

I looked down Pulver now and saw my dog exiting the chow's driveway on her way home, looking businesslike with her tail up. Isobel said she thought the hamster had moved. It wasn't dead after all. Sophie looked asleep, white as an egg. The dog's nonchalance enraged me. I sipped my drink and thought about scaring the dog with the car, just nudging her into the ditch to remind her who was the boss, that the angel of death hovered over her shoulder too. I grabbed the car phone and speed-dialed the Saab.

Ellen answered. "Where are you?" she asked. "I'm at the ER. You said you'd meet me."

"I got delayed," I said. "We're on our way."

I gunned the engine. The dog trotted toward us down the middle of the street in the summer twilight. I could hear children's laughter, their taunts and shrieks. Down our street toward the cul-de-sac they were playing kickball, a game that seemed to go on all summer.

Isobel said, "Daddy, watch out for the dog."

"We'll be right there," I said into the phone. "I just have to take care of one or two things."

"How's Sophie?" my wife asked.

"She's asleep," I said. "Exhausted."

"I talked to your friend Lily," said Ellen. "I don't blame her. I don't even blame you. But you have to get out now."

I hung up, sipped my drink.

I had the dog in my sights. I was waiting for the twilight

to fade so I could safely call it an accident. For a naturally inquisitive dog it was a long haul down Pulver, what with the garbage cans out on the curb and miscellaneous piles of crap and urine markers to identify. I just hated that dog. Every ounce of frustration, anger, envy and resentment focused like a laser beam onto that dog. Of course, it was my wife's dog—maybe that was part of it. I just fed it, housed it, cleaned up when it vomited on the carpets, slept in a bed covered with dog hair, smelled of dog. I gunned the engine and inched forward, nosing into the middle of the street.

Isobel said, "Pinky's shivering. His legs are shaking."

"Pinky's a girl hamster," I said. I glanced over at the cage where the hamster was spasming her last, back legs outstretched, reaching for some unimaginable purchase. Lucky hamster, I thought. Found your reward.

The dog saw me coming. She was bending to sniff at the base of the Rexforths' County Waste can, then she sensed the oncoming Subaru and glanced up. I was just going to nudge her. I don't know what happened. Blackout, or something. My foot went right down on the accelerator. Isobel shrieked. Sophie started awake and braced her hands on the dashboard, her eyes wide with horror under that bloody towel turban. I hit the brakes. The tires squealed. There was a thunk as I went over something in the road. Then I kept moving, the car somehow processing sideways, which seemed against the physics of wheel alignment. I took out the Rexforths' mailbox with the passenger door, bumped up onto their brick-terraced perennial garden, and finally came to rest against the trunk of a pine tree.

Time to take stock, I thought. Slow down and take stock. Katie and Isobel in the back seat were on their knees looking out the rear window. Sophie was slumped against the passenger door, her turban undone, fresh blood welling out of the wound on her forehead. The passenger window glass was cracked and starred. I touched her shoulder, and she turned slowly to look at me. She had her mother's eyes, I thought. Unfriendly, calculating—that what-have-you-done-for-me-lately look. This is what marriage does to a person, I thought. In our case, it turned a warm, friendly, sexy girl into a calculating machine.

The cellphone started to ring, a homely sound amid the carnage. Sophie's eyes went up.

"Don't answer it," I said.

I snatched the phone from its holster and smashed the touch screen against the steering wheel eight- or twenty-odd times. Then I threw it out the window. The dog was sitting next to the driver's door peering up at me, wagging her tail. Maybe it was the dog's ghost, I thought. Behind us lay the flattened body of the Rexforths' County Waste can.

The engine raced out of gear, ticking furiously, like hammers. Wisps of smoke or steam curled from beneath the hood. All around, the ruins of civilization, the end of the world as we know it.

"Wait here," I said, pushing through the door.

The Sun Lord and the Royal Child

I went to see my friend Nedlinger after his wife killed herself in that awful and unseemly way, making a public spectacle of herself and their life together, which, no doubt, Nedlinger hated because of his compulsive need for privacy, a need that only grew more compelling as his fame spread, as success followed success, as the money poured in, so that in later years, when he could no longer control his public image, when it seemed, yes, as if his celebrity would eclipse his private life entirely, he turned reclusive and misanthropic, sought to erase himself and return to the simple life of a nonentity.

You will recall that Nedlinger began his career as a so-called forensic archaeologist specializing in the analysis of prehistoric Iroquoian ossuaries in southwestern Ontario, and it was then, just after finishing his doctorate, that he met Melusina, a mousy undergraduate studying library science, given to tucking her unruly hair behind her ears and wearing hip-length cardigan sweaters with pockets into which she stuffed used and unused tissues, notecards, pens, odd gloves, sticks of lip balm, hand lotion and her own veiny fists, her chin depressed over her tiny, androgynous breasts. In those days she wore thick, flesh-coloured stockings and orthopaedic shoes to correct a birth defect, syndactyly, I believe it is called. Only Nedlinger, with his forensic mind, could pierce the unpromising surface, the advertising as it were, to uncover the intelligent, passionate, sensual, fully alive being hidden in the shadows.

A paradox: as Nedlinger's notoriety waxed, Melusina all but disappeared, growing ever more waifish and anorexic, tottering about pathetically on those high heels he made her wear, along with the short skirts and neon spandex tank tops; but as Nedlinger's fame touched the stratosphere (the money rolling in) and Nedlinger himself, unable to abide mass acclaim, turned increasingly cloistered and eremitic, Melusina began to seek the public eye, launching herself into a series of escapades in order to attract attention, courting rock stars, media types and wealthy party people, exactly the sort Nedlinger had spent his life avoiding. So that when she died, it might be said that Melusina's public persona had nearly eclipsed Nedlinger's or that Nedlinger was almost as well known for being Melusina's husband as he was for his own renowned work as a so-called forensic archaeologist.

As far as I know, Melusina was unfaithful to Nedlinger with only one other man, despite all the innuendo and gossip. When she died (the word *die*, in this context, is nothing but a euphemism for that horrid, public act of self-cancelling), they had no children, due, I believe, to a tragic injury Nedlinger suffered in a tractor accident as a boy on the family dairy farm near Burford, Ontario; the place is now preserved as a not-for-profit organic vegetable operation in his honour even though Nedlinger himself remembered it only as a typical Ontario family farm, a locus of sorrow, frustration, inhibition, philistinism, narrow-minded judgment, stupidity, race-baiting, poverty, animal abuse, overwork, incest, and casual, daily violence.

His father was Neil Nedlinger, a name of infamy and universal opprobrium, and his mother was Pearl Broadnax Nedlinger, a waspish, termagant enabler of the worst sort, given, I was told, to drinking Alberta vodka from the bottle and a lifelong subscriber to *Reader's Digest*. Nedlinger himself affirmed that throughout his childhood the Holstein-Friesian cows in the milking herd and a dog named Saturn were his only friends and companions. Oddly enough, Melusina revered Nedlinger's parents, a fact that enraged Nedlinger, who could only lock himself in his study when Neil and Pearl came to visit, turning up his favourite Cape Breton fiddle music to full volume to drown out the tinkle of teacups and drone of cheerful conversation filtering obscenely through the soundproofing.

When I went to visit Nedlinger that day, I had already been an intimate friend for twenty-odd years, dating back to the first glimmer of his fascination with the mysterious Southwold Earthworks complex, Canada's Stonehenge, our Great Pyramid, the Iroquoian Palenque, near Iona Station on the north shore of Lake Erie, where he did the work that eventually made him world-famous, a darling of the glamour set, rich beyond imagining. Nedlinger, a graduate student with goggle eyes, a huge body and long flapping arms and legs, clad always in his trademark coveralls and clodhopper boots, would often show up unannounced at our farmhouse door to examine the baby Indian skeleton my father had exhumed while putting in the foundation for a milking shed in a corner of the property adjacent to the archaeological site.

We kept the bones on display in a glass case on the dining room table, still half buried in a shovelful of sand, discoloured with a dusting of red ochre, a white bone pendant dangling from its fleshless neck and somehow caught in the fingers of its right hand as though the baby had been playing with it at the moment of death, a tiny, decayed moccasin dangling from the remaining toes of the left foot. The dead Indian baby, soon to be known as a result of forensic research as the Royal Child, fascinated Nedlinger, who would sit for hours at the table with his camera and notecards, staring at the diminutive skeleton, snapping pictures, occasionally jotting down an observation or wiping away a solitary tear.

Later, during his reclusive period but before Melusina's spectacular and grandiose suicide, he used some of that untold wealth, earned from practising forensic archaeology, to buy the farm next to ours, claiming that he believed there was a hitherto-undiscovered ancient ossuary on the property. I was still living with my mother and father at the time, two immortal, or so it seemed, hell-hounds, typical southwestern Ontario troglodytes who considered Iona Station next thing to Paris, City of Light, and drank instant Nescafé laced with Alberta vodka from morning till night, and believed themselves, practising United Church communicants, to be seated at the right hand of God and smarter than any university-trained forensic archaeologist or their own son, for that matter, who, though untrained in forensic archaeology, had nonetheless absorbed enough of the techniques from his master to have made personal discoveries adding a footnote here and there to the prehistory of the province, accomplishments that drew only cruel hoots of derision from those people who were closest to him and bound to support and love him unconditionally. "Who do you think you are?" my parents would sneer. "Another Armand Nedlinger?"

Nedlinger once told me my parents reminded him of his parents, and it was true that Melusina also idolized my parents, just as she doted on Nedlinger's parents, and would sit in the kitchen drinking Nescafé and Alberta vodka (which they called *tea*) with my parents while Nedlinger and I measured and remeasured the dead baby Indian's cranial dome and took samples for radiocarbon dating and DNA analysis, until one day, out of pure spite or perhaps due to some hitherto-undiagnosed dementia, my mother tipped the dead Indian baby, glass case and sand into a plastic garbage bag and sent it to the town dump.

At this time, there existed a peculiar tension between Nedlinger, already a world-famous forensic archaeologist, and his web-footed, non-practising librarian wife Melusina (even I, who knew her best, never saw her read a book); you could tell that they hated yet adored one another, that they fed on a symbiotic antagonism, completing each other in some malign but hugely productive fashion. She had fled to Toronto to escape the stifling mediocrity of suburban Thunder Bay City, a region of endless, tedious lakes, muskeg swamp and spruce forests, where her parents frequented country-and-western swing-dancing bars, rode mechanical bulls and drank Alberta vodka coolers laced with crème de menthe, which they called *tea*. Now only her alcoholic brother is left in the decaying family bungalow from which he manages an online gossip and innuendo site devoted to famous forensic archaeologists. The site is called *Digging the Dirt* and prominently displays digital photographs taken with a long-range lens of voluptuous coeds who often assist at forensic archaeological digs. The implication is that Nedlinger prefers this sort of student worker over the male kind, or for that matter the plain-looking, small-breasted kind, and in fact he does prefer them, although the camera has never caught him in frame with one of these girls. On the other hand, I have had to sue Melusina's brother twice to get myself Photoshopped out of compromising pictures.

I tell you this so you understand the kind of hell Melusina was escaping and why she was so eager to hitch herself to the rising star Nedlinger had already become even as he was cleaning up his doctoral thesis and preparing for a post-doc year at Berkeley, and why she threw herself at him despite the obvious inadequacies in her self-presentation. Of course, the truth was that in running away to Toronto she only found an exact replica of the life she had left behind in Thunder Bay City: country-and-western swing bars masquerading as chi-chi Queen Street bistros and so-called art connoisseurs who drank Alberta vodka at so-called art events, covertly referring to it as iced tea or bubbly, exactly the sort of cultural events I had disdained at Iona Station, the endless philistine and drunken bacchanals known as The Iona Station Historical

Society, The Iona Station and Port Stanley Curling Club, and the ineffable Senior Citizens Contract Bridge Club of Iona Station, a crypto-fascist anti-tax cabal, where the denizens drank Alberta vodka and accused each other of suffering from early-onset Alzheimer's disease while plotting, in the usual fashion of ethnic Ontarians, against artistic expression of all kinds, sexual freedom, freedom of speech and forensic archaeology, which threatened their moribund, self-satisfied little lives with revelations of an Edenic woodland world, home of lithe, smooth-limbed Indian maids and hunters who practised bucolic sex in the chaste underbrush and raised their cheerful, well-adjusted children in communal longhouses while worshipping beneficent sun gods.

Melusina wanted, as did many young people wishing to escape the cultural malaise of suburban Thunder Bay City, not to mention Iona Station and places like Burk's Falls and Omeemee, Ontario, to become rich and famous as a librarian, become the darling of a sophisticated international set she was sure existed beyond the dank, steaming spruce forests of Thunder Bay City, known formerly as the twin cities of Fort William and Port Arthur, although, in the event, she only managed to become the wife of a famous and wealthy forensic archaeologist (she organized Nedlinger's personal books and magazines according to the Dewey Decimal System), and as a result immersed herself in his shadow, becoming adept as a promoter of her husband's work, hosting exactly the kinds of superbly catered, hideously expensive soirees and dinner parties that Nedlinger abhorred yet required to advance his career as a forensic archaeologist; indeed it has been said that were it not for Melusina Nedlinger's work would never have achieved the mass recognition that propelled him into the A-list of world-class intellectuals.

I went to see Nedlinger after she died, as I say, when he was recuperating incommunicado at the farmhouse where, increasingly as his fame burgeoned, he had sought solitude and silence; there was no television, no telephone, no cellphone signal, no Internet and no mail delivery, circumstances that Melusina complained of relentlessly when, as was her habit, she hiked across the intervening fields to visit me—now alone after the sad passing of the old folks, who had died tragically in a barn collapse deemed unsuspicious by a coroner's inquest. No one answered when I knocked at Nedlinger's door, but I let myself in, as usual, calling, "Hallooo!" and combing room after room until I found him in his bedroom, stretched on the counterpane in Carhartt coveralls and Greb Kodiak farmer boots caked with mud, listening to Cape Breton fiddle music with earphones, his hands folded neatly and chastely over his protuberant belly. His eyes were closed and the volume turned up; he did not notice me at first.

A desk buttressed the wall, littered with a half-dozen laptops, stacks of books and the latest forensic archaeological magazines, page corners turned down or marked with festoons of multicoloured plastic flags, marmalade jars full of pens and highlighters—also several containing foreign currency (labelled)—mousetraps, plates with sandwich remains, drink glasses empty or half filled with cloudy fluids, the sharp smell of onions in the air mixed with mildew (there were shelves on three walls, stacked with more books, and several leak spots in the ceiling); the floor was strewn with stone implements (arrowheads, augers, knives, axe heads, adzes), potsherds, bits of bone, neatly tagged but helter-skelter, so that there was nowhere to walk.

I glanced at the exposed beams, the steel hooks (the previous owners, a couple of retired grade school teachers from Toronto, had apparently practised some sort of S&M role playing) from which, ghastly as it seems, Melusina had suspended herself, expecting, the story went, Nedlinger to arrive momentarily from the kitchen with his nightly Scotch and soda, a mistaken assumption as it turned out, because instead of padding up the stairs with his drink, Nedlinger, on the night in question, had paused in his study, taking out his magnifying glass to examine photographs he had made of the Royal Child, the very same dead Indian baby that had long lain in its sandy cradle inside the glass case on my family's dining room table in the farmhouse next door. Something had occurred to him, some doubt about his earlier theorizing, for he went to a bookcase and began to reread his book on the Southwold Earthworks, the story of the extinct, possibly legendary Neutral Indians (not what they called themselves), the famous sun-worshippers, deer-herding warrior-farmers, destroyers of the Fire People and the Cat tribe south of Lake Erie, soon to be destroyed themselves by marauding Seneca and microbes transmitted by the Jesuits.

While Nedlinger perused his old work, now in its thirty-seventh printing with multiple translations and world-wide distribution—not to mention the feature film starring Nick Nolte as the Neutral chief (name translated as Sun, Sun

Lord, Sunshine, Ray Of Sunlight, Cloudless Day, Naked In The Sun) and Jennifer Lopez as Morning Rain That Comes After The Night Of Clouds From The Day Before In The West (I myself wrote a small paper on Neutral meteorology as evidenced in their naming customs; the winds in southwestern Ontario generally come from a westerly direction)—his wife was doing the herky-jerky above their marital bed before a live video camera, gasping, gurgling, wondering irritably where Nedlinger was as her violent twitchings intensified. At the obligatory coroner's inquest (Canada's answer to reality TV), there had been some question as to the couple's sexual inclinations, but since there was ample evidence in Melusina's diaries that Nedlinger had no sexual inclinations (see tractor accident *supra*), this line of questioning proved fruitless.

Among other unpleasant and hitherto-unsuspected (by the eternally unsuspecting Canadian public) discoveries, the coroner's inquest revealed Nedlinger's festering, nearly psychotic hatred of modern life and all things Canadian (how it disgusted him that UNESCO routinely listed the country as one of the top places in the world to live), how he increasingly dwelt in the distant past, the past of the Sun Lord, the Arthurian ruler of the enigmatic Neutral Empire, how he gradually came to identify with the Sun Lord (played, as I say, by Nick Nolte in the movie), whose epic doomed love affair with his sister (see long name above) spawned court intrigues, divisions and rebellions that fatally weakened the nation, leaving it vulnerable to foreign invasion, heterodox religious proselytizers and disease.

It seems that in his cups or in moments of psychic breakdown due to the stress of maintaining his position as a world figure and notable forensic archaeologist, Nedlinger actually believed himself to be in touch by ESP or some other alchemical emanation with the Sun Lord; worse, he sometimes believed he was the Sun Lord reincarnated as a so-called forensic archaeologist, and this is how he knew that the dead baby my father had discovered in expanding the milking shed was not just any Neutral child but the very offspring of that mythic, aberrant union between the ancient Sage King of the Neutrals and his sister, the trembling, voluptuous, savage beauty known to us as Morning Rain That Comes After The Night Of Clouds From The Day Before In The West.

The inquest also brought to light the embarrassing fact that Melusina and I had conducted a brief, tempestuous affair while we were undergraduates at the University of Toronto and Nedlinger was at Berkeley pursuing his earlier, less famous work on exhumation and reburial practices among the prehistoric Ontario Iroquois, a betrayal for which Nedlinger instantly forgave me at the time of the coroner's inquest, well knowing, I assume, Melusina's fatal charms, her insatiable lust, and the documented Canadian penchant for secretive, hypocritical, adulterous, compulsively polymorphous sex congress (one of the main reasons, Nedlinger thought, that the country never really got ahead of its puritanical neighbour to the south despite having all the geographical and historical advantages).

This affair, as I say, was brief, amounting to practically nothing on the scale of such things. To be perfectly honest,

I did once throw her over the hood of a silver Lexus IS in the Bedford Road Municipal Parking Lot down the block from the Royal Ontario Museum, tore the crotch out of her panties and rogered her like a Holstein-Friesian bull, tears of happiness pouring from my eyes, her orgasmic shrieks filling my ears; in her frenzy she ripped the windshield wipers off the car and employed them to belabour my innocent shoulders. I do not know if my lust was driven by fondness or the universal human desire to hammer the lover of a more successful friend. I do not know if she used me or I used her or whether or not there was ever a glimmer of love between us. At the time I had no idea what love was, believing only that Nedlinger knew, and I envied him for it, envied him with a blind hatred that expressed itself as lust for his inamorata, the fair Melusina.

As I say, this affair was trivial in nature, barely worth mentioning, a minor blot on Melusina's prismatically loyal adoration of the famous one, although, as was admitted at the coroner's inquest, she and I did relapse once or twice, a handful of times at most, not, as Nedlinger's regrettable lawyer insisted, "obscenely fucking nearly continuously in front of my client's nose for the last twenty years" but, yes, as in being compulsively if not to say violently drawn to one another in a wallow of resentment, hatred, lust, rage and envy such that to this day I think all those emotions are love, are beneficent, are, in fact, the only species of grace the Lord can vouchsafe the losers of the world. At the end our lovemaking degenerated into a perverse parody of passion: I would fondle her webbed toes then ejaculate, dribbling my thin sperm onto those fishy fans of translucent flesh while she watched, touching herself, squirming in an ecstasy of humiliation, self-disgust and hatred. (Both Melusina and I joined Sex Addicts Anonymous at various times; for me, it was a good place to meet new women.)

I tell you this in the spirit of full disclosure, as they say these days, a phrase of hypocritical cant that discounts the existential impossibility of full disclosure, of knowing the true dimensions of the human heart, its capacity for pain, corruption, obsession, and deception. I tell you this so that you can understand my motive in going to visit Nedlinger some months after Melusina's death, after fortifying myself with several shots of Alberta vodka. I wanted, yes, purely human things such as closure, intimacy, unconditional love and revenge. I wanted Nedlinger's forgiveness and I wanted to torment him, favour him with lurid descriptions of the lustful spasms I shared with his wife (albeit in a compulsive nexus of bitterness, despair and jealousy), spasms that he himself had never been able to enjoy, wounded as he was (that tractor incident) and lost in the mysterious and ethereal world of his own researches at the very limits of forensic archaeology.

He had been like a god to us, distant, incomprehensible and untouchable. In truth, the fame and money had never meant much to him, and that made his success all the more aggravating. Now events had brought him low, his trajectory declining into a more human orbit where disappointment, lost love and death shamble among the survivors. It was in the twin spirits of *schadenfreude* and *ressentiment* (the patron spirits of our desperate, dystopian age) that I ventured tipsily across the fields dotted with scaffoldings, mounds of earth and half-filled trenches—old diggings, long abandoned—to visit my friend Nedlinger. (And I thought, staggering past those gaping wounds, how in Nedlinger's desire to uncover secret depths he had forever missed the surface of things.)

As usual, when I found him, he did not notice me at first, the eternal afterthought, the toady, the hanger-on, which only enraged me even more. (I was never a man of large spirit, I admit; I am the son of my parents, a shallow, envious, unachieved southwestern Ontario farm boy incidentally touched by greatness, an experience from which I have yet to recover.) I ripped Nedlinger's headphones off with a sweep of my hand. His eyes blinked open in surprise, then clouded with confusion and disappointment. I tried to speak, but words failed me as they always had. I began to weep. He placed his paternal hand on my forehead, a kind of benediction, and said, "Lennart—" (My name is Lennart Wolven, not that you need to remember it.) He said, "Lennart, I have terrible news for you"—words that made no sense since, prior to coming to visit Nedlinger, I had spent hours and days priming myself to deliver terrible news to him, confessional revelations of illicit sex congress with his now-dead but revered Melusina, and yet here he was consoling me for some hitherto-unlooked-for apocalypse.

He gazed at me sympathetically and, swinging his legs off the bed, sat upright so that our knees touched, took my wrists in his hands, made a curious *tsk, tsk* sound with his tongue, and said, "I was wrong, Lennart. All along I was wrong. Here—," he said, handing me a crumpled printout. "Read it yourself."

His resemblance to the actor Nick Nolte in this moment was extraordinary, and of course he knew I would be unable to read the statistical gobbledygook, the drone work, albeit the very foundation of forensic archaeology that had always escaped me—genomic sequencing, radiocarbon dating, counting the rat bones in a garbage dump. Even now this was his way of putting me in my place.

"It's the DNA analysis for the Royal Child," Nedlinger said. "It's finally come through. It took years because the samples were infinitely small and, after the first results, deemed corrupt. But we ran the tests again and again, always with the same outcome, until, over time, we came to believe them." He sighed, his chest heaving convulsively. "Besides, the procedures have improved. Read it. It was not the Sun Lord's —" He broke off, clearly in the throes of some deep inner struggle, the truth, it seemed, being too much for him to speak aloud. "It was much more recent, not prehistoric, not even Native."

"Jesus," I said, gasping. Ever the master of dramatic situations, he had me in thrall. The implications were obvious: the whole of Nedlinger's research, his fame, his personal fortune, had been founded in error. This was far more important than Melusina's sorry demise; I felt a white-hot nub of triumph in my gut, the heat slicked through my veins like a drug. "I'm sorry," I said, meaning not a word.

But Nedlinger continued, gripping my wrists in his huge, spatulate hands. "There can't be any doubt now," he said. "It was your mother's child, a fetus, born near term, abandoned and buried in a field. Your brother, perhaps. It happened to be buried at the edge of the ossuary, bits and pieces of artifact got mixed up in the grave. I should have recognized this, but I was blind with ambition. You know how it is, I think."

I don't know what I looked like, a staring wreck, in trousers forever too short and a cardigan sweater stained with coffee, a bow tie askew at my throat. I heard the words with uncanny clarity and thought, Of course, he's right. I thought, I knew it all along. I grew up in the House of Atreus, where children were consumed like canapés. I had a brother, but my envious mother slaughtered him, an epic act of negation to blight my life. No happiness for little Lennart, that was the rule. Betrayal, meanness and horror everywhere. My triumph evaporated. I had toppled Armand Nedlinger's world, shattered his version of reality, and now he had returned the favour. I was tranquil in the cosmic justice of it all.

But then I wasn't tranquil. It should have been me, I thought, dead in the furrows, forever innocent and pure, while, in life, I had done everything wrong, followed a dark star, fallen in love with the wrong woman, failed, failed, failed. What kind of story was this? I asked myself. Some malign, entropic, broken-mirror version of the Round Table knights, Lancelot and Guinevere, Lennart and Melusina, destined to ruin everything they touched and foul the dreams of greater men. Or was it just a piece of sordid Canadian Gothic, dead babies under the hedgerows, shadowy adulterous unions in cornfields, thin-lipped murderous mothers forever drinking their Alberta vodka *tea* and kneeling in the front pew at the Iona Station United Church, whispering "Amen" and quivering in ecstasies of puny triumph?

"My father—" I began.

"I don't think he knew, Lennart," said Nedlinger. "His

archaeological enthusiasm, though amateurish, was never faked. He always thought it was an Indian child."

"He brought it into the house," I said. "She never said a word. Her own dead child on the dining room table all those years," I said, "until she couldn't stand it any longer." The horror seeped into my heart gradually, drop by drop, like acid, like truth. And then I thought, This explains everything: my childhood pleasure in torturing small furry animals, my homoerotic yearnings, my masturbatory fantasies about the Jesuit martyrs, my inability to form friendships, play team sports and date nice girls from Sunday school. I felt a grim satisfaction—I was sure things couldn't get worse.

But then Nedlinger said, "There's more." He said, "That's not all I have to tell you, Lennart."

His words came in gentle whispers, words scarcely breathed into the silence that stretched between us. I barely heard him, and what I heard found no lodging in my brain, though a chill went through me.

"What did you say?" I asked, blinking back the tears, ripping the stifling bow tie from my neck and throwing it amongst the tools and potsherds strewn on the floor. I thought, No, no, not worse, not more—

"There's more," he gasped, his face working inhumanly, as if there were tiny animals, rodents, scurrying beneath the skin. His lips curled malignantly.

"More?" I breathed hoarsely. The air in the room seemed to scorch my lungs, the walls bulged inwards, my ears screamed with the pressure.

"Melusina—," whispered Nedlinger, the word barely audible. "My wife was pregnant when she died. I kept it out of the inquest. It cost money. But all these Ontario coroners are corrupt. I've never met one who wasn't —"

"Whose baby was it?" I cried, my heart awash with dread.

"You didn't always come on her toes, Lennart," he sneered. "You two thought you were untouchable in your scorn. Hatred was your form of grace. It made you irresponsible."

I clapped my hands over my ears and began to hum Del Shannon's "Runaway," music from my youth, or perhaps my father's youth. It was as if a vast trap door had opened at my feet; beneath me was nothing but sky, the constellations oddly reversed as in a mirror; I felt myself dropping through. I felt more pain than I thought was possible for a human to bear, and suddenly I realized the truth of the Immaculate Buddha's teaching that all life is suffering. Human beings were made for suffering; that was our purpose on earth. We were superbly designed suffering machines built to withstand all manner of guilt, loss, failure and betrayal. I even felt a twinge of pride at our incontestable capacity for self-inflicted catastrophe. At least we are good at something, I thought.

And then I ceased to think. No doubt the circuits were overloaded. Even my purely human talent for suffering was deficient. Just to stop Nedlinger from talking, I picked up the nearest object from the floor.

"What's this?" I asked. "Where did you find it?"

Nedlinger's face softened then fused with clarity. He patted the bedclothes for his reading glasses then peered at the object in my palm. "That's a freshwater clam half-shell, *Elliptio dilatata*. The Neutral used them to smooth the insides of clay pots. See how the side is flattened, almost worn through."

"And this?" I demanded.

"Side-notched projectile point," said Nedlinger, seeming to find pleasure in the terse scientific descriptions. "Carved from opaque chalcedony, Early Woodland period. It's very beautiful, beautiful and functional, and almost eternal."

But I was relentless. I shook a polished axe head before his face. "This?" I breathed. "Tell me about this one?"

"They were a beautiful people," Nedlinger said, dreamily, all at once ignoring me. "They painted themselves with yellow and red ochre, colours of the sun, their bodies made of light. They thought they were descended from the sun. They tattooed themselves from head to foot with charcoal pricked into the flesh, figures of myth came to life as they moved in the firelight. The warriors shaved their heads except for topknots braided with shells and porcupine quills that flashed like horses' tails when they danced. The world was a holy place to them and they themselves were holy beings, full of drama and prayer. Their lives were prayers."

Nedlinger turned to me, his expression a mask of doubt and resignation. "Lennart," he said, "all that's left for us is to try to remember them. Was I wrong to devote myself to that?"

I shook my head numbly. I held a shoebox full of tagged items. I knew what they were; I didn't need to ask. Like Nedlinger, I had been digging them up and studying them for years. Polished bear eye-teeth with holes drilled into them for stringing, fragments of slate gorgets, stone net sinkers, bone needles, awls, bifacial chert blades, decorated potsherds. The minds that had made them long gone to dust, along with the noble Sun Lord, my innocent brother, my sad parents and the fair, web-toed Melusina, object of lust, never known for her true self.

All the passion, self-torture and emotional drama suddenly dropped away like flesh itself, leaving me nothing but the adamant, insistent fragments of memory that now seemed true and full of mystery. I remembered a sunny June day, the three of us digging beneath an awning inside the Southwold Earthworks, wriggling along on our bellies, sweaty and filthy, using trowels, dental picks and watercolour brushes to dislodge the tiny immaculate remnants of the past, carefully cleaning, cataloguing and photographing each precious discovery. Were we ever happier? I asked myself.

True, Melusina and I were flirting outrageously, but Nedlinger, already famous and beginning to resemble Nick Nolte, was cheerfully oblivious, or even acquiescent. And the misidentified Royal Child still grinned unbearably in its glass case on the cherry table in the Wolven dining room. But the camaraderie of the work flowed through us like an electric current, lost as we were, I see now, in curiosity and wonder instead of our own grubby needs.

"No," I said to my friend Nedlinger, "you weren't wrong." And then, "About that, I mean. But doesn't it bother you that you were wrong about the Royal Child? That you'll be a laughingstock? Nothing but celebrity gossip and innuendo?

A week's worth of jokes on the nightly talk shows? Then a nonentity, zip, zero?"

"Something to look forward to, isn't it?" he said. "We could just get on with the digging." He sighed and heaved himself up from the bed and reached for the old canvas rucksack he had always carried to excavation sites packed with plastic specimen bags, notebooks, extra batteries for his camera, a dental kit for fine excavation, a magnifying glass, a Swiss Army compass and a pocket GPS unit, twine for pegging out site grids, and sandwiches wrapped in foil.

He said, "Lennart, there's still light. We can walk the fields the way we used to with Melusina. There are places we haven't looked."

I delayed momentarily, stunned by the sudden turn of events, the reversal of all my judgments, and the mysterious vectors of grace.

I said, "Wait a minute." Inured to my own darkness, I wanted to resist, object, find fault (just like my mother and father).

I remembered one luminous moment: Melusina chirping happily in triumph, holding up between her thumb and forefinger a fragment of clay pipe with two faces incised around the bowl, sombre, thoughtful faces, intricately lined with tattoos, her own face smudged with sand and ash from the pit she was excavating, her blouse charmingly misbuttoned and soiled, her eyes bright with excitement.

In the distance, I seemed to hear the earthy thud of hide drums.

Then I heard the slap of the outer door as Nedlinger burst through.

Suddenly stirring, I called out, “Yes, yes, Armand, I’m coming.”

Through the bedroom window, I could see sunlight shimmering on the pocked fields.

I shouted, “Wait for me.”

A Flame, a Burst of Light

Of the reasons for our lengthy and fatal sojourn inthe swamps of Sandusky, there are several theories. 1) The Americans wished to exact vengeance for atrocities committed by C^apt.^ Crawford's Indios on the Raisin River. 2) The Americans wished to prevent the men from rejoining their regiments before the close of the summer campaigns. 3) To supply the want of souls in the afterlife.

We were seven hundred dreamers starving and shivering to death in this gateway to the City of Dis.

Of the reasons for our deaths, there are no theories. Ague, fever (quartan, intermittent and acute), and the bloody flux carried us away. Old wounds, opened from damp and lack of common nutriment; pneumonia, dropsy, phthisis, galloping consumption, gangrene and suicide accounted for the rest. An alarming number of walking corpses attended the fallen like Swiss automatons in a magic show, then tottered off to expire face down in the bulrushes.

In the swamps of Sandusky, there were more corpses than souls. We had a surfeit of bodies. They were difficult to bury in the washing ooze.

Kingsland and Thompson, wraiths and daredevils, murderous on the day with Springfields we borrowed from the Americans at Detroit, mounted amateur theatricals though much bothered at delivering their lines on a stage of sucking mud. Sgt. Collins, of Limerick and the 41st, took the female roles, warbling a sweet falsetto. I mind he scalped Kentuckians with his razor at the Battle of the Raisin, along with Tenskwatawa's unspeakable Shawnee.

At Long Point in October, when we land, whaleboats and cutters rowed ashore by Negro slaves with superior airs, a barefoot girl in a wedding dress skips down the cliff path after regimental medical wagons and surgeons on horseback. Overnight, mist froze on the sails and sheets and shattered down on us like broken glass. We skate on the slick decks as the ships slide by the dunes and ponds along the point, mysterious and blood-red from rotting sedge and fallen leaves.

The cliffs are dun-coloured clay banks undermined by the fall storms with great half-dead pines like ships' masts toppling down and thin cows and hobbled, multicoloured horses grazing on narrow zigzag paths, low roofs and chimney smoke from a cluster of mean log and slab board houses above. We watch the girl, brown as a monkey, with ankles flashing beneath her dress, eyes wide at the sight of us. Preceding her, the medical wagons are like mastless ships with their iron kettles, great stirring spoons, and boxes of spirits and medicaments clanking listlessly. Clouds of geese and ducks, their wings flashing, lift and swirl over the point and settle again behind us.

I think of rhumb lines and wind roses and portolan charts. I imagine a map that indicates the vast populations of the dead, the departed souls like smoke spiralling up from the cemeteries, cities of corpses, suburbs of despair. The bodies of the newly dead make mournful humps of the sailcloth shroud spread over the deck. The boats roll and creak dolefully in the cold rain.

There are women among us, taken with the baggage at Moraviantown, who have lost all delicacy and shame due to the general deliquescence of bodies but yet display a pathetic dignity while voiding with the men or caring for their loved ones.

Except for a lucky few, we are all languid and ethereal, almost fleshless, pure soul, distilled by the elements and long steeping first in the Camp Bull prison and then the Sandusky swamps by Lake Erie (shoreline of ill fate). We all suffer tormina and tenesmus associated with the flux. We gripe and strain and evacuate little balls or blood or pus and then evacuate again, thinking what a way to die.

Or we suffer the shivering chills, sweats and hallucinations of the ague.

Those who can lift their eyes to the grey cliffs and the medical wagons and mutter encouragement out of habit to the others. Some weep at the sight of the medical officers on exhausted horses plashing along the beach, other ranks in scarlet coats at the double, without arms, hardbitten veterans of long campaigns in France and Spain and Canada. Music on top of the cliffs, dried-up wild grapevines like nets or veins against the clay, exploding milkweed pods, and a spruced-up boy in an oversized homespun tailcoat with clodhopper boots, a red rag tied round his throat, loping down the track and jabbering to the brown girl in the wedding dress.

There is a girl in my boat dying, left behind by a husband in the Provincial Dragoons who went down at Sandusky before our fatally delayed departure, went down in the water, shaking himself to death and weeping in his girl's arms, terrified to die, cheeping for his mam, the girl overcome with adoration and embarrassment for him and running away to shit when her guts cramped so that she was away when he died and in despair—half dead herself from despair—when she returned to find the camp gravediggers already wrapping him in a canvas shroud they used over and over to preserve the dignities.

She is beside herself, shaking with the ague or shock, no pulse, almost a ghost, not a tear in her egg-like eyes, sunk in the dark socket of bone and lash.

As we are all beside ourselves, stumbling trinities of I and not-I and the world beyond that presents only a curtain of sensation, all fluffs and billows like a linen sheet next to an open window in a gale.

We have the Americans to thank for enlisting us in the army of saints, yes, to thank for our education in asceticism and otherworldliness, for helping us to disentangle ourselves from the flesh as the desert hermits of old, our immediate state of dis-ease being a sign of something invisible that beckons.

In Sandusky, the energetic and the mad used their hands to dredge the swamp and construct islands for sleeping and standing, and there was some attempt to keep up drilling in a shallow pond otherwise a home to bustards and ducks.

Sgt. Collins, always the wit, said, "I don't wish to die and go to Heaven. I have a fear of heights."

I report to Surgeon Kennedy of the 41st, whose dun stallion, name of Clarify, knocks me over in its prancing. Kennedy leaps down, striding along the sand, chewing a clay pipe with a goat and horns on the bowl, ordering fires built, the kettles on, stooping to speak to the prisoners, making signs to his aides.

Already soldiers walk up and down with fresh apples and knives, offering slices to suck, rain falling the whole time, cold and dismal.

"Peruvian bark is wanted," I say, breathless at keeping up, teetering on my pins. "Charcoal and laudanum to bind the bowels and for pain. And blankets, man, blankets. Dry clothing. Clear soup with blood and plenty of water and salt, shreds of meat, not diced, pulped vegetables."

Surgeon Kennedy, saturnine, gloomy, sees the body as a flame, life as an explosion. He nods and nods and quietly gives orders to his aides. He has a year at Edinburgh. I have no teaching at all but cut off a man's leg with a hatchet after the Raisin and sewed the flap with binder twine and, by God, he was strong enough to survive, which is as good as a medical degree. The rest is bedside manner and prayer, I believe.

"Not five in fifty will see active service again," says Kennedy, measuring the ruined men.

"For God's sake, don't try to bleed anyone," I say. "They'll go off in a nonce."

"And who might you be?" he asks.

"Surgeon's Mate Netherby, sir!" I say. "Of the 41st. I am a little altered in condition, not up to scratch. I tried to save as many as I could—"

"Good lord," says Surgeon Kennedy, a gleam of recognition under his scrutinizing brow.

"And brandy," I say. "I could do with a stiff toddy. Or something mulled, all hot with raw brown sugar, cloves and cinnamon. Have ye any cinnamon in the apothecary stores?"

"Go and lie down in the wagons," says Surgeon Kennedy.

The brown girl dashes from one only slightly animate bundle to another, dodging the skeletal perambulants who importune her with fatalistic courtesy.

"A mite to sup, Miss?—Have ye a hankee or a bit of rag for a blanket?—Hasty bint, ain't she? Always rushing about. —She's very clean. Never seen anything like it. Fancy she's just been to a wedding?"

Soldiers shake out blanket tents, anchoring them with bayonets, and one of the new-style canvas round tents, snapping the cloth like cannon shots, strumming the guy ropes with their fingers. Fires blaze, fierce with snapping pitch, roofed with spits and sides of beef, night falling and the fires like the hecatombs of Greece glaring on the cliff face. Everything quiet and efficient. Quickly, quickly, for the dead are anxious along the shoreline where the Lake Erie waves slap indifferently.

The fiddle music has stopped. A line of villagers troops down the S-curve of the wagon track where rainwater dashes in rivulets. Smell of meat roasting. The dragoon's wife lies in the sand wrapped in an officer's wool coat, her husband's busby, much trod upon and muddy, clasped in one thin, languorous hand. But for Sgt. Collins, who attends her microscopically, she would be dead already, has wanted to die.

Death has become an image of release from suffering. It beckons us all like a sultry lover, a whore in a basement cot, promising forgetfulness and release.

Her name is Edith, pronounced in the French way, *Eh-deet*. Her husband was a magistrate's son at York who enlisted in the dragoons because he could afford a horse and liked being above everyone else. But his death was violent, gross and humiliating. He was so full of bright life (a flame, an explosion). She loved the youth of him.

"I shall go to him," she said, quoting King David, "but he shall not return to me."

The brown girl falls to her knees in the wet sand next to a dying soldier boy and begins to pray. Her bumpkin husband, the tailcoat boy who followed her down the track, dabs at her hair with his red kerchief.

Sgt. Collins, heady with fever, leans down, his voice resolved to a hoarse croak. "Ye won't do him any good with that," he says.

"I am not afraid," she says to the tall, gaunt, black Irishman hanging over her.

"Ye should be," he says.

Then he says, "This one was from Cork, with a sweetheart named Red Brigid Delaney. He won't know the difference. Can ye be Red Brigid Delaney, or are ye a useless whore?"

You can see her mull this over. On the one hand, prayer and everything she's ever been taught; on the other, the murderous transvestite Irishman, with his body courage and practical pity. No one has ever seemed as alive to her in that moment as Sgt. Collins.

"I can," she says with a steady look.

She has suddenly changed from the wild child skipping down the track in the rain, the near horizons of house yard and stump fence obliterated. Always the mystery of the boundless mercury-coloured lake and the local stories of witchery, seer stones and underwater monsters attracted her.

I remember the firing squads at Camp Bull along the Scioto where the river runs in reptilian loops by ancient mounds the provenance of which even the Indians have forgotten. Camp theories are divided as to their being raised by Egyptian or Phoenician travellers or whether they were remnants of once-great indigenous civilizations now gone to dust.

Geography reminds us that each fevered and urgent moment of meaning will pass and that the wind of time is a cancer that destroys us all.

Four American deserters in dress uniforms, bottle-green coats with black facings and shakos trimmed with braid, standing at attention like tall green candles (explosions of light) with their backs to the lazy river and their coffins, painted black, open before them.

One man harangues his executioners, another sags at the knees then recovers, a chest heaves, puffs of smoke spit ragged down the line, the musket reports drift over the broken ground to the curious prisoners, the speaking man jerks, his shako topples neatly into the coffin. One man jumps up shrieking. The reserve squad steps forward smartly and shoots him again, yet he lies there still living, his body twitching and heaving till the blood is all out. The others rest quiet. Steam rises from their wounds. It is a chill morning. Mist rises from the river.

Next spring the freshets will drag the coffins out of their graves along the riverbank, necessitating reburial.

At this stage, we have not begun to go off in great numbers. Our guards die as often as we do. Yet death is always an event of note, a mass execution being a dramatic occasion, a theatre of fatality, death as entertainment and diversion.

The camp hospital was at first chock full of the detritus of two lost battles, Erie and Moraviantown, the wounds of the lake fight being the worst: bodies smashed under falling spars or loose cannons rolling along the deck, wounds filthy with shreds of sail or wood splinters, lads waiting patiently to get their bits cut off and then turning themselves out, like candles snuffing, equally patient, quiet as lambs.

It gives you vertigo to think. Everyone's life is a centre of a universe that evaporates at the moment of death.

But I do love a neat amputation.

And we bury our dead in the Indian mounds, mixing their bones with the bones of ancient men.

Sgt. Collins stumbles into Surgeon Kennedy, both reeking of spirits. Kennedy has stripped to his shirt in the rain to operate, every gesture spare and perfect and strong. His body a furnace, the damp steams off his shoulders. He pokes lint stoppers soaked in gin up his nostrils to combat the stink, steeps laudanum in a teapot, tipping the spout to his lips from time to time.

Collins wears his pantomime frock, burst at the waist, grey with filth.

Kennedy: "Sgt., why are you dressed like that?"

Collins, reeling: "With permission, sir. Not my colour, I know, sir. There was a want of blue taffeta in the camps. Cruel treatment for a poor industrial wheezer like me, sir."

Kennedy: "Yer a bold squireen, Sgt. Collins."

Collins: "Nought can touch me now, yer honour, sir."

They are old friends from fights on the Ohio shore and at Moraviantown, when things went south for us, but Kennedy orders Field Punishment for the sake of form. Five strokes with his wrists bound to a medical wagon. Cut down, Collins drops on his knees, shakes himself like a dog, then staggers back to the sick looking refreshed, the flame inside burning fierce and hot.

At the Battle of the Raisin, Collins was on detached duty with Capt. Crawford's command, Shawnee savages dressed in scraps of stolen American uniforms, with Springfield and Kentucky rifles, hatchets and knives made of stone, sharper than razors. He conversed with Tenskwatawa and drank home-brew whiskey with the Potawatomi skin-changer Crippled Hand, men whose style of bravery was mystical and unearthly cruel.

He was like Saul dancing among the prophets, and when he returned, he was not the same.

"I am not afraid," the girl says.

"You should be," says Collins, more strange than human, more alive than the rest of us. "I am conjoint with Death," he says.

The brown girl's soldier boy dies at her breast. For an hour she commits adultery, becomes his lover, vows she will meet him in Paradise, kisses his cracked and infected lips, whispers dirty endearments in the shell of his ear where her tears catch, and presses his lank, algorific fingers between her legs to warm them.

She forgets herself in her pity, gives everything fiercely, a strange, grim joy in her heart.

She knows she has become a guide to the Land of the Dead. She knows the way.

Her present groom, centuries behind her in his naïveté, looks sickly with the recognition of the unknowable risen up in the heart of his gamine lover. A pot roast man, clever with his hands, no imaginative throw, dull as a trivet.

She covers the boy's face with a blanket tail and turns to the next.

The first man she helps evacuate makes her gag, but she cleans him gently and thoughtfully, pouring hot water from a kettle, washing herself in the lake.

S$^{gt.}$ Collins blows on a horn spoon dripping blood soup, picks out the solid bits with his fingers, and lifts Edith's head on his arm. Her thin blue lips refuse to open. But her eyes widen in fright. She does not want to be brought back.

"I shall go to him," she whispers.

The rain is turning to damp, feathery snowflakes.

I limp past the horse lines, climb into a canvas-topped wagon out of the rain, and nod off sharpish after wriggling into a sailcloth bag lying close to hand. Smell of sawdust and rotten meat in my nostrils, two coffins stacked on end, peaceful as a grave.

Wake up when they start to pile fresh corpses above me.

A drummer boy with a pencil and a list, look of terror on his face, says, "You b'aint dead."

I am paralyzed, wedged in, the wagon suddenly crowded with fatality. "I'm not dead," I say, testing the hypothesis. Corpses like cordwood on either side and on top, stiff and cold. I recognize old comrades, including Kingsland, the amateur thespian, hugging me in his bare blue arms, teeth bared in a snarl of rictus. The icy skin of a dead man is always a surprise.

"You were talking," the drummer boy says. "I was sheltering and I heard voices in the dead wagon. I thought the dead was talking."

"Can you get me out?" I say. "I'm really not dead."

"I told you," he says.

I crawl out of the dead wagon in time to watch great steaming drays lean into the incline as the first drafts of returning prisoners ferry up the cliff track and off on the road to Burlington, where there is a real hospital.

There was another boy, just like this, shot for a deserter at Camp Bull. Out for a ramble, he got lost. A friendly innkeep said to stay the night and he'd vouch for him in the morning. But the innkeep hotfooted it to the camp and turned the boy in for the reward.

The firing squad wept. The boy awaited the sting of the musket balls with a look of weary disdain, disgusted with a world that had failed to live up to his expectations.

At the Battle of Lake Erie, we had farmers, distillers, printers, tanners, tailors, cobblers and carriage makers to sail the ships, with the usual result. Moraviantown was a rout. We made a stand at the Thames River, but our hearts weren't in it because everyone knew we were only saving the General's coach and baggage. The Kentuckians marched up in waves and fired at thirty yards, mostly missing us, but we broke notwithstanding, the savages in the trees on our right fighting on gallantly to cover the retreat till Tecumseh fell, the last honourable man in British Canada, by which I mean a fool.

S^gt. Collins and the one-day bride hover over Edith, the beach being depleted of all but hopeless cases.

The girl's nipples stand up like acorns in the rain.

Collins thrusts his hand into the fire. His eyes roll up

white. Smell of burning hair. When he takes it out, it glows but is otherwise whole. Some parlour trick he learned from the wabeno warriors.

He says, "I'll be dead in a month. I have the sight."

Fires still blaze, souls blaze, the cliff face glimmers like the walls of a crypt under a ceiling of darkness. Wisps of mist drift in off the lake.

Surgeon Kennedy rests on a fish rack, tapping his clay pipe against his teeth, eyes smouldering with exhaustion and despair. Bodies not flames any more but skin bags, all the same on the inside, bone and gut and blood, fragile as a bubble. The face a thin mask of identity, the soul a hopeful mystery.

In his laudanum dreams he sees himself commanding the rearguard against Death and the intrepid Black Imps of Satan. But he's tired of fighting.

Edith bears herself in silence. You can see her thinking fiercely. There is much to remember, much to tally, going toward the Gate.

I shall go to him, she thinks, but he shall not return to me.

Sgt. Collins minds me watching, calls me, "Here, Lazarus," like a dog.

I think there's an earthquake but then notice I am trembling violently with ague. I note the telltale horripilation of the skin.

I am hallucinating, or the place seems tremendously holy. You can reach out a hand and touch the Other World.

A kindly apothecary's mate of the 41st, someone I once knew, wraps a blanket over my shoulders and bids me come closer to the fire. But I want to watch. I am already nostalgic for the yeasty richness of life, its sudden turns and dramas, its deep sadness, its mysterious and gorgeous purposelessness.

No one knows why Collins cares for Edith, but he is sudden and belligerent and understands by doing, not thinking. He accepts what he cannot parse, doesn't mind that he will die, despises pain but doesn't fear it, and thus is completely at home in the world.

The girl from the clifftop feeds him soup while he chafes Edith's hand. She fears only that this moment will end, afraid she will be left to change her dress and become a wife. For her too, action has leaped beyond what she can know. She thinks all life must be quest for style.

An hour before daylight, a dreadful, somnolent calm falls upon the beach. Fires down to embers, the living, dead and dying blanketed lumps in the sand, one or two, still awake, stare at the glowing coals.

The girl says, "It's my wedding night." She pulls Collins down beside the jacent Edith.

Only one person has an eye to see, sleepless for fear he will sleep and die.

In the morning, a white rime of frost blankets the sleeping and the dead. The lake is still as ice.

Edith's skin is like the lake, translucent, blue and cold.

I shall go to him, she thinks.

Surgeon Kennedy presses her eyelids shut, thinking how she has attained invisibility (a flame, a burst of light) and a higher knowledge.

S[gt.] Collins draws a uniform from stores, hangs it over his bones, whistles through his teeth hefting a new Springfield and a bayonet, tools of the trade. He is a man happy to have enemies, a regular Jonathan among the Philistines, and the Americans are so handy and numerous.

We blink, we wake up, we are in Canada, we are among the living.

It's not so much, state of anticlimax, chilly, damp, vexing people.

The sunlight over the lake is like milk.

In Sandusky, we were in the company of saints. We thought God was in the worms and maggots that ate the dead. Smoke blasts from the horses' nostrils. Soldiers in red jackets (embers, flames) blow on their hands, kick sand over fires, piss against the cliff. The chinking of harness sounds cheerful and mundane.

The girl in the wedding dress takes a seat in the wounded wagon. Her face is pale, pinched, fierce and proud.

At the top of the track, as the wagons trundle through the village, the girl's husband strides along beside, waving his bandana like a pennant, begging her to get down. But she doesn't answer, doesn't look.

Remnants of a wedding, slab tables in a stumpy field, clusters of wild asters in pots, a flag, a spit and a smoking ash pit.

She takes one final glance at the slate expanse of the lake, landscape of unease, imbrued with qualities that contradict reality.

At the last sorry log house, where a loyal Canadian pig roots in a garbage heap and another stands at the open front door, the husband stops and shies a rock at the departing column, face crimson with fury.

Five men of the 41st silently fall out, stack their muskets and chase him down among the houses, beating him unconscious with their fists.

Two weeks later, Sgt. Collins volunteers to go slaughter more Americans and dies (a tongue of flame, explosion of light) leading militia against the Kentucky cavalry at Malcolm's Mills. It is said the Canadians panicked and broke, leaving him on the field, where his body was much abused by Kickapoo scouts.

Of the girl, nothing else is known.

INTERMEZZO

MICROSTORIES

The Ice Age

Dead of winter. Snow falling for days on end. Snow up to the rooftops. School cancelled. The yard is as bright and blank as a computer screen.

The children and I climb onto the roof with plastic shovels. We carve a fantasy of crenellated walls marching along the eaves and over the peak, with watchtowers at the corners and a gate with snowmen for guards. It takes all afternoon. We dangle a pair of my undershorts from a rake handle for a flag. We name it the Castle of Narth.

At night, the neighbours come over, and we climb the roof with camp chairs, sleeping bags, and down comforters and crouch around Coleman lanterns, sipping Swedish vodka inside the castle walls, watching shooting stars between the drifting clouds. The children toss tennis balls for the dog, who leaps off the roof with its ears streaming, then swims back through the snow like a seal.

The Snivelys have not been getting along of late, the usual tectonic drift of marriage. She says the snow makes her think of Eskimos. She asks did we know that Eskimo men share their wives with strangers, and looks at me. Snively swan-dives off the roof, then climbs back with a lopsided, embarrassed grin.

The next day, it snows again, almost silent except for the infinite whispers of flakes. City plows block the driveways, then vanish to concentrate on the main streets and arterials. By consensus, the drone of snow blowers goes into remission. The children burrow tunnels between houses, constructing elaborate mazes where they play hide-and-seek and ambush the dog with snowballs. Snively's boy Mose and the Czernik girl, both high school seniors, lose their way, switch off their phones, and canoodle in a forgotten hollow.

My wife discovers a bag of votive candles and says, "These might come in handy." And then she says, "I wish Loreen Snively wouldn't look at you like that."

"Like what?" I ask.

"You know," she says.

We snap on cross-country skis and shush to the strip mall, dragging a toboggan for supplies, past brand new backyard skating rinks, golf-course toboggan runs, knots of red-faced, laughing children, regiments of snowmen. My wife sticks out her tongue to catch the flakes, which makes me want to kiss her for about eight hours.

That night, the TV forecasts Arctic Clippers and blizzards. Pundits speak earnestly of a new Ice Age. But the Internet rumours of power outages in the North, vanished towns, wolves appearing on the city outskirts, have more the flavour of UFO sightings than anything real.

My wife climbs the roof and lights candles along the castle walls. The castle looks like a fairy tale, a dream of fire, blazing up against the falling flakes like a bubble of light.

The neighbours arrive with pots of stew and torrents of mulled wine. We sing campfire songs and golden oldies and watch the children nodding in the lamplight, hot in their synthetic down and microfibre cocoons.

Loreen Snively says her dreams the night before were disturbed by men in fur returning from the hunt, flinging down carcasses of polar bear and seal, and having their way with her. Snively says we ought to start planning hunting parties, maybe train the dog to sledding. "You never know," he says, trying to look prudent and manly in his faux rabbit fur Mad Bomber hat.

My wife cuddles with our eight-year-old against me. She gives a little shiver, though she can't be cold.

We watch the candles on the castle walls gutter and go out.

The Poet Fishbein

After the incident in the commuter jet restroom, the poet Fishbein found a new career counselling troubled teenagers in a Staten Island halfway house, in part to fulfill his court-mandated eight hundred hours of community service but also because he genuinely enjoyed working with young people, seeing himself in every bad boy with spiked hair, tats, stainless steel tongue ball, and purple eyeshadow. One evening, Fishbein and a half-dozen residents were doing ecstasy in front of the fireplace as a cheery fire consumed cheerily the last of the maple-finish kitchen chairs, when the new staff volunteer, Reguiba Placentia, a recovering crack addict, sex worker and early childhood education professional, exploded through the door. "What the fuck is going on?" "Group therapy," said Fishbein dreamily. He found Reguiba, whom he had never seen before in his life, strangely familiar and mysteriously attractive. "Are you the guy who set his shoe on fire over Minneapolis?" she asked. Fishbein decided it would be better to use mental telepathy to explain to her the complicated situation involving the joint that flared up and scorched his moustache, how he simultaneously dropped the joint and jerked his head back, knocking himself nearly unconscious on the commuter jet restroom mirror, how the joint somehow became entangled in his sneaker laces, causing the plastic trim to smoulder and, yes, emit some noxious smoke, which Fishbein didn't really notice at first because he was trying to see if his head was cut by spying in the mirror through his peripheral vision, how finally the smoke alarm sounded and things suddenly became truly confusing—the words "shoe bomb" and "terrorist" came into the picture in ways he had yet to understand completely. After explaining all this telepathically, Fishbein realized Reguiba was still waiting for an answer, so he pointed to a pale, limp, neurasthenic, semi-conscious boy named Julian and said, "That would be him."

The Night Glenn Gould Played "Chopsticks"

The woman in 314 has a walleye, claims to have suffered a spiritual crisis when she was fourteen that led to bleeding from her palms and feet, claims also to have once lived in Glenn Gould's apartment building in Toronto and heard him playing "Chopsticks" one night from the roof, claims also to be a witch.

Tell the press I am unavailable for comment.

Don't be afraid, I tell myself. None of the things you fear the worst will come to pass.

Glenn died at the age of fifty, I am fifty. When I was thirty-three, I couldn't get over the fact that they crucified Jesus when he was thirty-three. It's the same with Glenn.

Buddy

Buddy is seven and sweet and fat and slow to speak like his dad and a latchkey kid of long standing and considerable resources since his dad is gone and I work two jobs to keep the household floating. Days, I work as a teaching aide for the special-needs kids at the elementary school, and nights, I work a flex shift transcribing medical dictation for the pediatric clinic. Days, Buddy goes to the elementary school, and when he's done he walks home and plays *Halo* on Xbox and eats Cheetos and macaroni and raises more fat cells. I am a responsible mother, but aside from making enough money to meet the house payments, also the phone and electricity, and keep him supplied with macaroni and Cheetos, I haven't got time for much else. One weekend I took him to the beach, but he complained of sunstroke and West Nile virus and said there were dead things floating in the water. Another time we tried hiking at the state park, and Buddy lay down on the trail claiming dehydration and snakebite when we were still in sight of the parking lot. I blame my husband for taking off like that and living on the other side of the country with another woman named Millie (she is really nice and a Christian and was married to our pastor before the trouble). And then I blame myself for being too proud to take him to court and make him pay me to keep Buddy. I thought I could handle everything myself, a moment of hubris and lack of prudence I might now reconsider, though no one else will. I have a degree in classics from a respected college and a thirteen-year-old Volvo that Buddy's dad left instead of love. And a house with payments and a dog named Phanto of nondescript breed and personality. We live in the most Christian state in the Union, where churches and golf courses are the most common landmarks. The only fun I have is watching amateur porn sites on the Internet and playing with myself under the covers late at night when Buddy is asleep. This is not much of a life for a girl, let me tell you. But I console myself that it is only temporary. Soon Buddy will grow up and learn to take care of himself (or else he will become the state's responsibility). By then I will be across the Great Divide and on the downhill slope, waiting for breast cancer or some other such mercy, and death will put an end to this long regret.

Hôtel des Suicides

The girl looks familiar, and over sherry in the afternoon I admire the partial nudity of her skull, the pierced flesh, the rings in her lip.

She reciprocates, alluding to my eye patch, which on this occasion I have remembered to wear.

She knows nothing of her past, thinks "the war" is something that happened in Iraq and that we won it. She has a self like window glass, believes that irony is imperialism, threw a balloon inflated with her own blood at a mounted policeman in front of what she thought was the American embassy but was in fact a US Airways ticket office.

I tell her she reminds me of someone.

I look like you, she says.

Twins

My twin brother Buddy shot his best friend Richard Maliciwicz to death in the garage the year we were twelve. He has always regarded this as the turning point in his life, that things got better afterward. I never shot anyone. Consequently (according to Buddy), my life has all been downhill. I wanted to be an artist but wound up in computer call centres (of course, I've been on disability for years and have forgotten everything I ever learned about computers). I marked life's stages with nervous breakdowns—at age sixteen (the first time I had sex), at twenty-two (college graduation), at twenty-seven (marriage), at twenty-eight (divorce), and thirty-three (first job).

Buddy took a sociology course in college and will say things like, "It's a mistake not to think we're born from violence, that violence and sacrifice aren't at the root of the family and everything it stands for. I made myself the day I shot Richard. I'm not saying it wasn't hard on him. But we all need our Richard Maliciwicz." And it's true—Buddy has had a happy life. I find it shocking and mysterious how Fate has rewarded him. He enjoys a booming academic career with a well-paid consulting business on the side (he gives human relations seminars to large corporations). He loves his wife. They are raising two sons, ages eight and ten.

I admit it's unnerving to see the way he casually leaves his hunting rifle around the house. My heart stops whenever I'm over there and see his sons playing with the neighbourhood kids. "They might shoot me," says Buddy airily. "Or each other, or you." Sometimes I think he's insane. But I'm the demonstrable madman in the family, so my opinion carries little weight.

Splash

In the early days, when settlers first scraped out their meagre holdings along Lake Erie's north shore, it was not uncommon for fishermen to catch mermaids in their nets. Dumped on the beach, the poor things died quickly, their darting eyes turning to gelid orbs, their hair becoming brittle like coral as it dries, their pitiful cries dwindling as their gills gaped spasmodically for oxygen. Dead, they were more like pubescent children, with seahorse tails, triangular faces, pointed ears, translucent skin above their scale lines, and veins green instead of blue. I saw a preserved specimen once in the home of a distant relative whose ancestors had been slavers in the Caribbean before coming to Canada in the nineteenth century. The little corpse was exhibited in a green glass jar the size of a puncheon, suspended in olive oil, its tail folded up in front of its face, its eyes shut, its arms and hands crossed neatly over its breasts. There is a persistent Internet rumour that another individual, less well preserved, is kept locked in a vault in the basement of the Royal Ontario Museum in Toronto.

Xo & Annabel, A Psychological Romance

The second night, when it was clear that something was starting between them, Xo began to lie to Annabel, tiny lies at first, minuscule evasions, shy reticences. It was not only that he wanted to impress Annabel but that he yearned to be in love with the sort of woman who would fall for the kind of man he pretended to be.

Wolven

After they made love the first time, things got strange. He peeped through the window blinds, shook himself like a dog, and muttered something about the moon. Then he said, "You must chain me in the closet. Whatever happens, don't let me out. Lock the door. There's a deadbolt." She was drunk and naked and limbic, not thinking with her forebrain, something much lower.

"Then what?" she asked flirtatiously.

Little Things

I think—I believe—Elind is trying to kill me.

Little things.

The other night I woke struggling with a pillow over my face.

She said she was making me comfortable.

Last month I had severe stomach poisoning. When he pumped my stomach, the doctor said I must have eaten a bowl of Weed & Feed mistaking it for porridge.

Otherwise she is loving and attentive in the old way.

And I keep my suspicions to myself, not wanting to hurt her feelings. She likes to be needed.

THE COMEDIES

The Lost Language of Ng

According to the Maya, their grandfathers, the Ng, refused to assimilate with later civilizations but instead retreated, after a period of decadence and decline, into the southern jungles whence they had emerged. They are rumoured to be living there still, a hermetic and retired existence, keeping the Secret Names in their hearts, playing their sacred ball game, and copulating with their women to inflate the world skin bladder and supply the cosmos with ambient energy, the source of all life.

The last known speaker of the language of the ancient race of Ng passed quietly in his hospital bed at the Cedars-Sinai Medical Center in Los Angeles, where he had been flown the week before for emergency surgery. The cause of death was listed as "massive organ failure." He was 92 years old, according to estimates, though he himself claimed to be 148. He went by the name of Trqba, though he always said this wasn't his real name; it was "my name for the outlanders."

His real name, Trqba told researchers shortly before his death, was a secret, a secret so mysterious and terrible that were he to utter the name, the world would end the instant his breath stopped on the last vowel of the last syllable.

The Ng are believed to have been a proto-Mayan people who emerged, somewhat mysteriously, from the jungles south of the Yucatán a thousand years before the birth of Christ and established regional hegemony over the inhabitants of the dry central plains, impoverished tribes that lived by eating insects and grubbing for roots, given to war and venery but incompetent at both, according to Trqba (see C.V. Panofsky, "An Account of the Ng Creation Epic," *Proceedings of the Royal Society*, 1932). A carved stele discovered at the ancient Ng capital, long concealed beneath temple ruins, depicts the dramatic emergence of the Ng people, their great tattooed war god ____ stepping naked from behind a tree, brandishing a cucumber (or boomerang; listed as "unidentifiable" elsewhere) in his hand, his erect penis dripping blood (according to Trqba; according to Giambattista et al., 1953, possibly water, sweat, urine, semen, or "unidentified fluid") on a row of diminutive, dolorous, and emaciated natives who are about to have their limbs severed (see Farrell, "Ng Stele Recounts Imperial Conquest," *National Geographic*, 1951). The name of the Ng war god is lost because to utter even one of the eighteen divine diphthongs would have meant the sudden and cataclysmic end of life on earth. But Trqba (see Trilby Hawthorn, "New Light on the Ng, a Jungle Romance," *People*, 2009) said that the Ng referred to him in conversation using conventional epithets such as Snake or My Girl's Delight.

Soon after migrating out of the jungle, the Ng invented canals, roads, terraced agriculture, pyramids (prototypes of the stepped Mayan E type, aligned with the solstice and equinox), cannibalism, and the mass sacrifice of captured enemy maidens (also, poss. the wheel, the automobile, and an early computer-like device; see von Däniken, 1964; von Däniken believed the Ng were extraterrestrials from the planet Cephhebox). They built immense cities with central plazas surrounded by the usual towering stone temples and played a peculiar version of the Meso-American ball game at the end of which the winners would be bludgeoned with gorgeously carved obsidian death mauls—the losers would become kings and nobles. Since no one wanted to win (especially in the Age of Decadence, when the Ng Empire went into precipitate decline—between the years 7 Narthex and 27 Px on the Ng calendar), in practice the Ng ball game went on forever; players would grow feeble and die and be replaced by younger men, who in turn would be replaced, and so on. (See Proctor, "The Final 16: Ritual Roots of American College Basketball," *Harper's*, 2001.)

According to Trqba, the ancient Ng came to believe that the sacred ball game generated a spiritual current or life force (analogous to the Chinese concept of *Qi*; see R.V. Hemlock, "The Ng Generator: Prehistoric Experiments in Conductivity," *Popular Mechanics*, 1955) that kept the world dome inflated (like a skin bladder, a curiously foundational concept in the Ng metaphysics) and animated all living things, and that if the Ng heroes—oiled, naked, emaciated, arthritic, toothless, and decrepit—ever ceased their listless ebb and flow upon the court, the world would end catastrophically. (For the ancient

Ng, it seems, time was equivalent to constant motion with no linear progression, something like treading water or jogging on the spot; see Larios, *Changeless Change: The Ng Enigma of Time,* Oxford University Press, 1999.) Though he claimed to be the last of the Ng, Trqba paradoxically seems to have believed that somewhere deep in the jungle, on a rocky, weed-strewn court hidden by the overarching green canopy, men and boys, lost tribal remnants or even spectral reanimates, still played the ancient game, the score forever tied at 0-0.

He also said that the Ng kings and queens were required to have sex continuously, night and day, an intimate analogue of the ball game. When they stopped, he said, "the world will end." He himself, he claimed, was a descendant of the Great Kings and had "tired out" several women in his day. How the Ng chose their kings when no one ever won or lost the sacred ball game remains unclear; in practice, it seems, they may have been selected by lottery using the incised peccary knucklebones found in heaps scattered randomly around the ancient Ng cities. When the sexual prowess of the Ng kings began to wane, priests would dispatch them ceremonially in the night, catching them unawares and in flagrante, as it were, using the garrotte and those famous obsidian death mauls simultaneously. (For a lurid fictional account of the legendary erotic practices of Ng royalty, see Anonymous, *The Love Diary of Anaconda, King of the Ng,* Black Cat Press, 1963.)

Trqba was raised an orphan on the edge of a vast yam and cucumber plantation owned by a multinational conglomerate, where he earned his living as a farm worker from the age of five. Married, the first time, at twelve, Trqba converted to Christianity under the influence of a fanatical missionary sect based in Idaho and known as The Last Days of the Rising of the Great West in Christ. When he was sixteen, Trqba eloped with the young wife of Preacher Malachi and immigrated to the United States, where he resided for several years in Sea Hills, New Jersey, working as a school janitor. At the end of this period, Trqba's wife reconciled with Jesus, returned to her native Idaho, and went into couples therapy with Preacher Malachi. Trqba always claimed he had "tired her out." But the incident coincided with a vision of the Sacred Ng Ocelot Lord (real name unrecorded for the usual reasons) in the girls' changing room adjacent to the Sea Hills High gymnasium. (For details of Trqba's biography, see his Wikipedia entry, much of which is sourced to *News of the World* interviews with Rachel Malachi, his ex-wife, who alleged that Trqba was born in Sea Hills of Puerto Rican parentage, a claim that scholars have dismissed; see J.V. Oliveira, "New Light on the Last King of the Ng," posted to her archaeology blog *Picking Old Bones*, 2008. Note also that Trqba's sojourn in New Jersey corresponds to the liminal stage in the van Gennep sequence; see V. Turner, *The Ritual Process: Structure and Anti-Structure*, 1969.)

Trqba had no formal education and could neither read nor write, although he claimed to be able to translate the complex glyphs archaeologists discovered carved into the inner walls of the Ng temples. When asked how he knew the ancient language, Trqba said his grandfather had taught him. This is a common locution amongst primitive oral cultures, who view all older people indiscriminately as "grandfathers" and "ancestors." What is now known for certain is that upon his return to the Yucatán, Trqba hired a local medicine man and plantain farmer named Nunez de Vaca (Nunez of the Cow—not a sacred name) to teach him the ancient wisdom of the Ng. During this period, Trqba's half-American daughter Naomi supported him, earning their living as a surfing coach, burrito chef, and sex worker in nearby Cancún.

Nunez of the Cow schooled Trqba in the Ng creation epic, the famous Mlx Draf Ng'dal. (See the excellent Helwig translation, University of Toronto Press, 1995; a literal translation published on the Web in 2009 by R.J. LeRoi is infelicitous and a sieve of errors, e.g., "...he raddled them with his rapier Snake" [Helwig] v. "he hit them with a worm causing multiple puncture wounds and contusions" [LeRoi], and "sunlight struck sparks from his night-coloured death maul" [Helwig] v. "the sun was reflected off his brown stone hammer with a wooden handle" [LeRoi].) Trqba also studied numerology, the cyclical order of the years in the Ng calendar (Spot, Narthex, Rx, Nuht, and Px) and their relationship to Ng astrological signs (seven as opposed to the usual twelve) and astronomical observations (highly advanced, it seems, for the Ng priests were clearly aware of the recession of the equinox and other stellar arcana, including a concept very close to Dark Matter). He learned the names of the various medicinal plants in the Ng pharmacopoeia and practised decocting remedies in a homemade lab in a lean-to behind the house he shared with Naomi in the ancient Mayan village of Zarthapan on the edge of the Great Yucatán Sand Plain. (See Dr. Baron Rappaport, MD, PhD, MFA, "How the Ng Cured Cancer," *Modern Medical Bulletin of the White Plains Psychiatric Center*, 1967.)

Trqba also become an adept in Qx-Qx, the Ng martial art known for its unique combination of quietist meditation techniques and brutality. It is no secret that at this time he became addicted to narcotics and natural psychotropics, which he manufactured himself according to ancient Ng recipes and sold to tourists. Nunez of the Cow taught him the usual shamanic repertoire of non-rational metamorphic practices: shape-changing, time-travelling, and flying. Using secret drugs and Ng breathing exercises, Trqba claimed to have maintained an erection continuously for three years and "tired out" five successive young lovers, local village girls noted for their robust appetites. He learned the Secret Names telepathically while sleeping off a six-day bender on a straw mat in Nunez of the Cow's summer kitchen (but, of course, went to his deathbed without revealing them). One story, perhaps only a rumour, has it that he was bitten by a deadly fer-de-lance while communing with the gods in a ruined stone sanctuary hidden in the jungle, and the snake promptly died in agony. At the University of Michigan's Rudolph X. Hartshorn Archives, there exists a scratchy recording of Trqba singing a primordial Ng war song, a tape made by the noted American folklorist Wendel Bateman in 1952. Bateman died soon after while attempting to reproduce the mystic Ng art of cliff-jumping under Trqba's tutelage. (See T. Wilberforce, "The Curse of the Ng: NEH Halts Research Grants Following Mysterious Yucatán Deaths," *New York Times*, May 10, 2010. The *Times* puts the number of dead or hospitalized since 1950 at fifteen, but unofficial estimates are much higher.)

Battle Song of the Ng Host

I have copulated with the bodies
Of the enemy dead
I have copulated with the ocelot
And the jaguar
And the tree sloth
And the garden slug (possible mistranslation).
Yea, I have slain them with my spear-snake-thing,
Have impaled them on my righteousness.
Their women have groaned with envy
And thrown themselves upon my terrible spear-snake-thing.
Yea, I have made love with Death,
And her children are the glorious Ng
Whose every word is poetry.

—Helwig translation

In later years, Trqba followed a more conventional and abstemious lifestyle. After Nunez of the Cow's death in 1973, Trqba continued to study the Ng language and lore through dreams, astral projection, and the use of psychotropic drugs, which, he said, was the traditional method. (He claimed that the more achieved Ng intellectuals and members of the priestly class eschewed speaking altogether and communicated by "signs and thoughts." See Boris Napkin and V.I. Urpanzurov, "Some Thoughts on Sacral Communication among the Primitives of the Yucatán Desert," *St. Petersburg Philological Review*, 1982, wherein the authors dispute Trqba's claim, insisting that the Ng actually possessed two languages, one High language, complex and poetic, and a Low language, or Ngian demotic, for the common people; no one actually spoke High Ngian since to utter a single syllable would instantly bring the world to an end.) He was adopted by the "chefe" or Lord of the rare (possibly extinct) Yucatán hairless marmot (*Cynopius sesquipedelia*), a diminutive yet vicious mammal with neurotoxins in its saliva, known to eat its paralyzed victims alive, which became his tutelary spirit and totem. Trqba married three more times; all his wives eventually left him, satisfied but "tired out," he said.

In 1998, he received an honorary doctorate from the University of California (Berkeley) for his contributions in the fields of anthropology, translation, archaeology, cancer and AIDS research, sexual dysfunction, poetry, and the War on Drugs. It is believed that at this time he had a brief if unpublicized affair with the famous Hollywood starlet C____ D____ (her name cannot be revealed, not because the world will end, but because of the threat of lawsuits; see C____ D____ v. *Vogue Magazine*, currently in the Second Appellate Court, State of California, docket #7384-2903). This claim is surprising given that by his own count Trqba was 125 years old. It must also be observed that he was never what one would describe as an attractive man. When he died, he was no more than five feet tall, with three remaining teeth and skin the colour and texture of a walnut. All his life he affected a pencil-line moustache like some early twentieth-century cinema Lothario. He was an incessant smoker—American Spirit cigarettes when he could get them. He wore baggy trousers to accommodate his priapism, a mismatched suit jacket, and a straw fedora stained with ancient sweat. Yet he was a proud man who carried himself like a young cockerel or a king till his last illness, despite the incontinence, the paralysis in his lower limbs, the constant moist, hacking cough, and the glass eye which he often turned inward so that he could, as he said, see himself better.

Let it also be noted that Trqba never spoke Spanish with the facility one would expect from a lifelong practitioner. He spoke English with a New Jersey accent, but he did not speak it well either, not as a native. He often remarked to researchers that Ng was the only language in which he felt at home, that every other language seemed prosaic, inept, incomplete, and foreign, that in Ng the world was a beautiful and dramatic arena for the practice of love and war. Nor could he ever convey in English or Spanish or any other contemporary language the true complexity of Ng thought, which required the full thirteen distinct genders, twenty-five tenses, and the dozen moods (including the hopeful-but-not-optimistic mood) of High Ngian. The Ng had 433 words for the English word "thought," which can only be translated in clumsy, agglutinated phrases, e.g., the thought that goes in and out of my head like a fly in a jar, the thought that comes when my lover undresses in the moonlight by a still lake, sad thoughts as I watch my enemy die upon the field of battle while I hold his hand to comfort him. Common conversation was highly abstract and philosophical; Ng children were taught the arts of war, mathematics, poetry, and love from an early age. According to Trqba, it would be impossible to translate the English sentence "I need to take the car to the garage for an oil change and pick up the dry cleaning" into Ngian, even the demotic vernacular. (See Hilo Revlog, *The Incommensurability of Universes: Ng Syntax and the Weltanschauung*, Universidad de la Rioja, 1998.)

To be sure, many scholars dispute Trqba's claims and the body of research that has grown up around them (for a survey of the current literature, see Magot, Vetch, Weeder, and Wurmes, *The Ng, an Anthropological Fantasy, a Counter-Proposal*, University of Nijmegen, 2010). His account of killing five men in spectral duels on glacier-covered Yucatán mountaintops with the Vulture Eye of Ng must be disregarded, just as his "lifetime" tally of 5,363 lovers only weakens his credibility as a scientific observer. It is undoubtedly difficult to overlook Trqba's unmistakable air of charlatanism and shoddiness. He was raffish, lewd, intellectually inconsistent, and maddeningly mysterious (all, it might be added, traditional characteristics of the shaman; see V. Shklovsky, "The Disreputable Intermediary: Signs of the Mystic Other in Daily Life," *Readers' Digest* online, 2009, a revision of his earlier blog post "Our Saviour was a Hippie Magician," posted on the now-defunct *Delta Alert for Alien Invasion*, 2008).

In March 2010, as he lapsed into a mysterious lethargy symptomatic of his final decline, Trqba dramatically recanted all his previous Ng testimony. In an e-mail to his friend and noted paleolinguist Boris Napkin at the Stalinski Philological Institute in Belarus, Trqba disowned a lifetime of teaching and the immense corpus of research and translation he had generated, saying that Ng wisdom could only be transmitted in the ancient oral mode from priest or "grandfather" to acolyte, in the language of High Ngian in the midst of outrageous feats of ritual asceticism and endurance in the lonely wastes of the Yucatán desert. Written down (or, as the ancient Ng would say, "made to lie still in the snow like corpses"), Ngian words lost their capacity to generate Being and became nothing but utilitarian devices of crude communication. He said to Napkin: "How can I teach you what I dare not speak?" (As per his usual practice, this e-mail was sent by Trqba's beloved Naomi, companion and soulmate; their incestuous relationship has long been a subject of fierce underground debate in the otherwise tepid purlieus of Ngian Studies.)

The week before he died, despite the grievous nature of the impending surgical intervention, Trqba was excited about the trip to Los Angeles. He wanted to see the "famous footprints" in the Hollywood sidewalk and shop on Rodeo Drive for "cow-boys" boots. But he seemed very tired just at the end, a little wistful. Before he lapsed into a coma, Trqba became delirious and seemed, yes, to speak in tongues, even to prophesy in the magisterial tones of ancient royalty. The sounds he made were meaningless to observers, but one, at least, switched on his pocket digital recorder on the assumption that Trqba was speaking in true Ng. Alas, the device malfunctioned. (The resulting forty-nine minutes of digitized static are available on YouTube.com, erroneously tagged "signals from Cephhebox.")

A Paranormal Romance

Everything Starts at a Bookstore

I was supposed to meet Zoe for dinner at a chic Parisian restaurant she had discovered on the Internet, a crucial rendezvous during which I intended to propose marriage. But I was running late. A fierce, cold rain lashed down as I bounded up the metro steps, rain as I had never experienced before. It drove me back into the underground, where dozens of African Parisians discussed the weather in languages other than French. I glanced at my watch and leaped up the stairs again, blinded by the torrents of rain.

Wind whipped the leafless plane trees along the avenue. I spotted a flower shop and ducked in, thinking to buy a bouquet for my love. But I must have slipped through the wrong door, for I found myself in a neat, closet-like second-hand bookstore with dark oak shelves marching back toward an ancient desk fortified with parapets of leather-bound tomes. I hovered, dripping, in the doorway, loath to enter and perhaps spatter valuable books with water but also reluctant to dive back into the deluge. I wiped rainwater off my watch face, frantic with vexation and indecision. I naturally blamed all my troubles on the Parisians, their precious City of Light, and Zoe's love of travel, which I did not share.

At length, an elderly gnome, about three feet high, with white braids wrapped like wheels at the sides of her head, shuffled from behind the desk in what looked like wooden clogs. Everything smelled of dust, mildew, and creosote. Her skin was the colour of ash. The high ceiling seemed wreathed in smoke. She dragged anciently toward me, taking hours it seemed, with a small book clutched in two veined and corded hands the colour of mahogany. She extended her arms, offering the book to me, almost toppling over as she held it out, her blue lips working wordlessly, foam at the corners of her mouth. But her watery blue eyes darted intelligently, anxious and beneficent.

A folded slip of paper fell from the book as I reached for it. Then I had to grasp the old crone by the shoulders to prevent her from falling as she vainly tried to catch the escaped sheet before it landed on the damp floor. I could already see the blue cursive letters soaking through the yellowing page. I snatched it up by a corner and flung it open, hoping to preserve the message, but the letters were beginning to run. The penmanship was bold, what used to be called copperplate; the words were, surprisingly, in English. They disappeared as I read them. "I adore you. I belong to you for eternity. It doesn't matter what you have done. I take your sins for my own. I will suffer the punishment and happily wait for you in the Afterlife. But, my heart, if I could just see you once more before I go, it would be so much easier to bear. At the Gare at seven under the clock."

There was a wormhole through the paper. The ink was pale with age. The book was Lautréamont's *Chants de Maldoror*, an early edition, in French, of course. I had never read it. The aged dwarf was on her way back to her desk. It would take her a week. The rain had stopped, replaced with the sepia twilight of Paris in late autumn. I looked at my watch. It was a quarter to seven, just moments before I was to meet Zoe, my future wife (and dental hygienist). A strange feeling descended on me, the feeling of being directed by an unseen hand.

At the Gare

It occurred to me that Zoe was always late, that I would be cooling my heels, eating bread at the table alone while the waiters crossed their arms and whispered about me behind my back. The Gare du Nord was not far. The craziness of the impulse lent it an air of spontaneity and romance. The note was a hundred years old, if not more. What Gare did the writer intend? What city? Still, I was the reader of the message and it wouldn't hurt me to fulfill the ancient invitation. I knew that in some obscure way I would think better of myself for having done so.

I dove down the metro steps, interrogated the route map on the wall, and raced to the platform, catching the train as the doors swept shut. The trip seemed interminable. I wondered about the handwriting, the person who wrote the note, for whom it had been intended, what crime he had committed, what terrible fate awaited her. Already I was haunted by the thought of the lovers who never met, their not-meeting whispering down the decades till the moment when the leaf of paper fluttered from the gnome's hand. At that moment, I realized I still clutched the book. I had not paid for it.

I raced up the steps at the Gare du Nord and burst onto the concourse. It was, yes, just seven. Now I would be well and truly late meeting Zoe. She would arrive unsupported, puzzled at not finding me at the table, embarrassed to sit by herself. I had imagined I'd find some nineteenth-century pedestal clock with Roman numerals for numbers and thick arms black with coal soot. But there was only the huge digital sign, DÉPART DEPARTURE ABFARHT, blinking destinations in waves like wind blowing across fields of wheat. Everything smelled of marble and ozone. Fresh rain fell in waves on the glass roof as if we were under the ocean. Trains gleamed impatiently between pedestrian *quais* where the globe lights walked into the distant dark. There were the usual chic-looking French people hurrying along with their black-rimmed glasses and baguettes like loaded rifles, also students with haversacks and Muslim women in head scarves. I waited under the digital sign, looking at my watch, feeling a little foolish. Except for me, everyone was in transit, passing through, with a definite destination in mind. An African sweeper with a barrow came by, emptying the trash. Except for the public address system blaring incomprehensible messages at me in French, I was engulfed in silence.

I opened the book and read the words "*Plût au ciel que le lecteur, enhardi et devenu momentanément féroce comme ce qu'il lit, trouve, sans se désorienter, son chemin abrupt et sauvage...,*" which were incomprehensible to me yet somehow seemed to find an echo in the passionate intonations of the public address announcer. I noticed a slender, melancholy figure emerging from the shadows at the rue de Dunkerque entrance, cloche hat, black lipstick, dark wool coat down to her calves. I noticed her because her eyes were fixed on me, and I could feel them. She was unique, it seemed, in a train station packed with what you would expect, and I had no doubt that it was she who had left the note for me in the book of poems (printed in an unreadable language). But as soon as I thought this thought, I realized how ridiculous it was. I remembered Zoe and the lateness of the hour and heard the clisp, clisp of the commuters' footfalls like dead leaves falling all around me.

The woman seemed dangerous, tragic, sad, and fascinating. I was having the adventure of my life just watching her stride across the concourse. She came toward me like Fate, ferocious and wild. I felt in my jacket pocket for the little velvet box that contained the engagement ring. Zoe would be in a panic. I was the anchor of her little world. I felt a twinge of contempt for that little world. I had answered the invitation, the lover's call. The woman was wearing strange wooden shoes, *sabots*, I think they are called. I wondered how I knew that. Her eyes were blue, fierce with certainty and renunciation, also relief, the deepest happiness. I looked for the exit. I knew I could escape. But what was there to escape to? She broke into a rueful smile. I could smell book dust, mildew, and creosote. Under her cap her black hair was braided in tight wheels against her temples. Her skin was white as paper. I held out my arms for her. Up close her hair smelled like snow, like winter.

"You came," she whispered, clutching my hand. "It's enough. Now I can endure everything."

"I don't know what you're talking about," I said.

"Je t'adore," she said. "It's all I need."

"Je t'adore," I whispered. (It did not escape me that all at once I could speak three words of fluent French.)

I knew she wasn't real, but I suddenly realized what it meant to say my heart ached, to know what I wanted and could not have. My entire life seemed diminished, something I watched on a TV screen, scripted, flickering, but nothing I was participating in. The revelation made me sick. A strange malady. I had the feeling that henceforth the years would be haunted with the realization that nothing could measure up to this moment and this woman for whom there would never be a substitute.

At the Café

It took me ages to find my way to the restaurant what with the metro suffering one of its frequent shutdowns (due to electrical shortages, or maintenance problems, or terrorist threats) and the snow falling, snarling the traffic. Yes, snow was falling. Suddenly it was winter. The streets were like strips of parchment. The gas lamps hissed as I walked beneath them. Horses dragging the street trams clattered on the pavement, striking sparks with their iron shoes. Nothing, of course, surprised me. I felt a certain posthumous quality in everything I did. I didn't recognize my clothes.

The café was boisterous, overheated, and brilliantly lit with gaslights and candles. Waiters in aprons, oiled hair, and black moustaches swayed amongst the tables. Women in little bonnets perched upon their upswept hair laughed coquettishly. I spotted Zoe almost at once. She was sitting with an earnest young man dressed in a modish grey suit, his hair already receding slightly, giving him an air of premature wisdom and solidity. Her cheeks were warm, her eyes vivacious. She wore a ring on her finger. They were drinking champagne out of fluted glasses, and their waiter was making a fuss, fluttering excitably around them—an intimate, everyday tableau. *Bonne chance,* I thought, trying out more of my new-found French, feeling a certain Continental contempt for the naive and conventional tourists.

I sat by myself where I could watch them. I ordered Pernod and a hot grog and asked for some paper to write on. I could smell winter through the window glass, astringent, bracing, and real.

Shameless

When she was eight years old, Megan Strehle conceived an unnatural passion for Tamas Preltz, a fifteen-year-old apprentice butcher in the town where her father took vegetables to the local farmers' market. She would beg her father to bring her along when he loaded his Ford half-ton pickup with cucumbers, tomatoes, potatoes, summer squash, beans, and Brussels sprouts. Then she would run to Roohan's Butcher Shop and stand at the end of the counter, shifting her weight from one foot to the other, till Tamas deigned to notice her. He could tell she was in love, and a meaty, stupid boy with a square red face, he took pleasure in being cruel to her. Sometimes he would pretend not to see her the whole day long. Sometimes he would entertain Roohan's fat daughter Rachlin by tossing bits of sausage in the air, urging Megan to catch them like a dog. Megan said, "Arf, woof," snapping at the flying sausage ends, revelling in the laughter, which she took as applause. She didn't realize she was the butt of their jokes; she thought it was nice of Tamas and Rachlin Roohan to include her in their games. But one day her father caught them at it and attacked Tamas Preltz with a leg of lamb that had been hanging from a hook in the window. When he had beaten the boy to his knees, he went to Roohan and paid for the leg of lamb, spoke a quiet word, took his shamed daughter by the hand, and led her away, weeping. Tamas Preltz was fired from the butcher shop. He packed his bag the next morning, gave notice to the Widow Hopkins, and left for the next bigger town along the railway line when the noon commuter train came through.

This should have been the end of the story, but passions had been let loose, hearts wounded. Megan Strehle turned against her father, grew angry and remote, neglected her looks, which were not much to begin with, and plotted revenge and escape. She put pillows under her skirts and walked around on market days proclaiming her pregnancy, naming Tamas the father. She stood outside the window of Roohan's Butcher Shop with her face against the glass till Rachlin appeared, then shook her belly at the fat girl and barked like a dog. "Arf, woof." She refused to help her father in the Brussels sprouts patch, left the chicken coop open for a fox, ogled the hired man, who was toothless and nearly sixty, and wrote terrible love poetry, which she recited from the dormer roof on moonlit nights. Her father tried to win her back with chocolate almond candy, hair ribbons, and preteen fitness tapes, but when she was twelve, she hitched a ride with an itinerant computer repairman to the next bigger town and searched high and low for Tamas Preltz. No one could remember the boy. It was as if he had never existed. When the computer repairman, whose name was Evan Ravit, moved to the next, even bigger town, she went with him. He taught her code and bought her chocolate almond candy and said that the universe was a symphony of binary numbers. They slept together like children, with their clothes on. Her parents believed she had been kidnapped and went on national television to beg for her safe return. Their pleas were so moving that they appeared on several important talk shows and, briefly, had their own Christian reality TV series, before her father went into rehab and ran away with a famous country singer named Halley Ratliff who reminded him of his daughter. Evan and Megan watched her parents' antics with embarrassment and glee. They changed their names to Mitch and Amanda Bunim, pretended to be brother and sister. Later they pretended to be married, and even later, in their innocence, they thought they were married.

Meanwhile, Rachlin Roohan pined for Tamas though she was older than the boy by eleven years and had had no more encouragement than the occasional laugh over the idiot dog-girl Megan Strehle. When it became apparent that Tamas would never return, she stopped eating, began to lose weight, and read romance novels in the cold storage room, wearing her mother's otter-skin coat and her father's deer-hunting boots. Soon she was thin and quite beautiful, but eccentric and fever-eyed. She went to the bar at the edge of town and slept with men she barely knew, still wearing her father's hunting boots and the otter-skin coat, with her hair flung wild on grey motel pillows in the sickly glow of neon lamps. Her father neglected his butcher shop in his despair over her behaviour, turned to drink, beat his wife (the innocent in all this), held dark colloquy with the bull mastiff watchdog named Edmundo, and eventually hanged himself on a meathook in the cold storage room. Some time after the funeral, a fat man with thin hair and a speech impediment took photographs of Rachlin with his cellphone camera, photographs that spread around the world on the Internet in a matter of hours. Lonely men in Mumbai and San Diego, smitten with the sad beauty, naked except for her hunting boots, besmirched with semen, smiling enigmatically, wore themselves to nubbins in masturbatory frenzies. The night the photos first appeared on the Web, a wave of suicides circled the globe. Legends swiftly attached themselves to Rachlin's mysterious photographs. From Vladivostok to Buenos Aires, men set out in quest of her, despairing, in thrall to desire, abandoning jobs, wives, children, and elderly parents. One by one they found her, knocking timidly or pugnaciously at her motel door at all hours, sometimes stumbling over one another on her welcome mat or waiting in line on a suite of folding chairs she kept on the parking pad. She slept with them all, hungry for something, she thought, something that not one of them could supply. And one by one they slunk away, failed, empty, and still despairing. Then came a little epileptic former third grade art teacher from Nairobi, a man whose Swahili name meant Field of Cows in English. Field of Cows failed also to satisfy the mysterious Rachlin Roohan but refused to give in to despair, though he had much to despair of, only asking to be allowed to stay near her and crawl into her bed when she was alone and make her hot milk and bull's blood toddies now and then. For her part, growing ever thinner and more beautiful on catnaps and a diet of bull's blood toddies, Rachlin Roohan barely noticed Field of Cows. She spent her days reclining languidly against the dirty pillows between bouts of lovemaking, staring at the rainy parking lot beyond the motel window, weeping sometimes at the thought of her dead father, trying to remember what Tamas Preltz looked like, vaguely anxious that she could no longer picture the man she desired more than any other. Only when Field of Cows fell into one of his noisy fits would she stir herself to help him, shoving a dirty slipper between his teeth to keep him from biting his tongue, hugging his arms to his sides till the flailing subsided, whispering sweet endearments into his ear. "Baby, baby," she would whisper. "Baby, baby."

Tamas Preltz never reached the next bigger town along the railway line. The train stopped briefly on a siding for the westbound freight. Three men, who had been drinking heavily in the bar car, stumbling back to their seats, suddenly conceived an immoderate passion of their own for this stupid, innocent-looking, blond butcher boy. They tied his hands and took turns with him in an unoccupied toilet, then tossed him off the train into a freshly manured Brussels sprouts patch beside the track. The three men, returning to their seats, grew rancorous and quarrelsome. They were guilt-stricken over the sudden access of an *outré* passion, which till that moment had been utterly alien to them. One wanted to go back and make certain Tamas Preltz was dead. Another wanted to confess to the train conductor and send for an ambulance. The third wanted to swear an oath of perpetual silence so that they could return to their wives, children, and jobs as though nothing had happened. "Life is full of secrets," he said. "Why should we be different from anyone else?" In the years that followed, one of the men killed himself in despair by driving his car head-on into a moving van carrying the furniture and personal effects of an immigrant mathematics professor named D'if Afghani and his thirteen children, one of whom had been accidentally packed with the family bedding and was later found uninjured amid the wreckage. The second man left his wife and moved to a large Midwestern city, where he opened a hobby shop catering to the shy, lonely inner-city boys and girls. And the third became a prominent Christian conservative politician. Meanwhile, the night of the train incident, an aged, blind herd dog named Rusty discovered Tamas Preltz unconscious in the mud and urinated on him. After regaining consciousness the next day, Tamas followed Rusty home and slept in his doghouse until discovered by a girl coming to feed her beloved pet one morning some days later. The girl would have screamed, but she was deaf and dumb, and her scream came out like the sound of wind in a pine thicket. In signs, Tamas explained what had happened to him. The girl wrung her hands and wept. She reached out and smoothed his dirty hair with her fingers. Transformed by misery and her tender, guileless pity, Tamas Preltz felt love for the first time and in that moment began to regret the way he had treated Megan Strehle. For his part, Rusty, the dog, was glad when Tamas moved in with the girl and her family because it had grown crowded in the doghouse and Tamas ate all the table scraps. Tamas worked for the girl's family, members of a vegan organic farming co-operative, and eventually married the girl, whose name was Laurette Vitapotle. They had two children and adopted two others when Laurette proved incapable of bearing more babies. She had grown obese despite a diet of Brussels sprouts, raw carrots, and hummus. But the fatter she grew, the more Tamas Preltz loved her. They would often embarrass other members of the co-op by making love in the field rows or behind a hay rick or beside an open window on moonlit nights, their cries of joy setting off mysterious vibrations in the listener, inspiring laughter, lust, and the desire for fat babies. But the co-op prospered, cheerful children gambolled in the vegetable patches, the Brussels sprouts and cabbages won prizes at the state fair, and tour buses brought doting crowds of vegan initiates to browse in the fields, where sometimes they caught a glimpse of Laurette and Tamas scampering naked or felt the pulse of their seismic lovemaking.

Years later, a grown woman with three children of her own, married to Evan Ravit, who had made a fortune selling erotic cellphone ring tones over the Internet, Megan Strehle, known to everyone as Amanda Bunim, discovered her husband in bed with an office intern named Pesh Afghani, a beautiful brown girl with a mathematical turn of mind and a strange story about once having been locked for days in a family linen trunk. "I'm in love with her," said Evan, now known as Mitch. "I've never known love before this." "That's funny," said Megan. "I'll go tell the kids we made a mistake." "She's a brilliant programmer," he said, "and she does the funky-funky dance with her bottom." Broken-hearted, Megan barricaded herself and the children in the east wing of the family mansion and sought a restraining order against her husband, although, in fact, he didn't need any restraining, indeed, spent most of his time playing table tennis with Miss Afghani or chasing her around the bedroom. Their cries of delight depressed Megan Strehle. She couldn't deny that Evan Ravit seemed happier than she had ever known him to be. And she remembered how he had picked her up on the road to the next bigger town all those years before, her belly lopsidedly swollen with a pillow, her tears running into an old sock she carried instead of a handkerchief, her heart bursting with love for a boy whose name she could no longer remember. (Her eldest son was, however, named Tamas, and she had long ago given up eating meat on account of some vaguely disagreeable memory associated with butcher shops.) Evan had offered her twelve-year-old self a ride out of kindness and empathy for her loneliness; he too was lonely, as only an itinerant computer repairman could be. She thought now that he was right, they had never properly been in love. And she realized she had always been lonely, even in Evan Ravit's arms. She found a vegetarian online dating service called Hearts of Palm and met sixteen gentle, sensitive, candlelit-dinner-and-long-walk-loving, whole earth, organic, environmentally conscious, horny men the first hour and settled on one named Darter who lived on iceberg lettuce, vegan turkey substitute, and generic-brand diet colas. He ran ultra-marathons, had lost an eye and a foot in a war, talked incessantly into a wireless headset, and said, upon meeting Megan, "Babe, I'm moving you out of the holding pattern onto the incoming flight path." "Who do you talk to on that headset?" she asked him. "No one," said Darter. "I just wear this thing so I won't be embarrassed talking to myself." Then Darter told her a sad story about how he had once seen the picture of a woman in hunting boots and an otter-skin coat on an amateur porn site, how he couldn't get her out of his head, how he gave up everything and spent thousands of dollars to track her down (somewhere he had a wife, a college-age child, and a toxin-laced but profitable electroplating shop), how he found her in a motel, attended by an ancient, diseased African, so thin she was almost translucent, how he made love to her and yet even in that moment of supreme triumph felt all the possibility of happiness drain away. Sometimes, he said, he returned to that desolate place and watched the men waiting to be entertained and then slipping away abashed, wounded, and lorn. He saw himself in every one. Megan thought he would do as an interim lover and invited him into her bed, where she tried to do the funky-funky dance with her bottom. But they both felt they were only going through the motions, both yearning for something else, as though sacrificing to distant gods, but the gods never appeared.

Tamas Preltz had forgotten Rachlin Roohan when he caught his nine-year-old son, Stalton Preltz, deaf and dumb like his mother, surfing pornographic sites on the Internet. The boy was staring at the dark, blurry image of a woman, naked except for a pair of hunting boots and an otter-skin coat thrown back to reveal her nether hair and breasts. Father and son were transfixed, barely able to breathe, and when they finally shook themselves awake, their eyes met in a moment of shared understanding. Tamas forgot about reprimanding the boy. He gently pushed Stalton away from the screen and took his place, still not recalling Rachlin Roohan specifically, only aware suddenly of something deeply buried and lost, the memory of a memory of an experience he had never had, of a woman he had never met, infinitely desirable, ineffably sad. He was disturbed presently by the sound of Stalton's weeping. The boy's eyes remained fixed on the screen, his hands tugging distractedly at the front of his soccer shorts as if pulling at some imaginary knot. The sight of his son suffering in the toils of a desire he had no way of understanding brought Tamas to his senses. The boy was trying to speak, his lips making a sound like wind in pine trees. Tamas switched off the computer and swept Stalton into his arms, whispering, "Shh, shh, my love," grasping the boy's hands in order to stop their obscene pulling. He rushed out, found Laurette washing Brussels sprouts for market, made signs to her to take the boy, then rushed out again, seeking solitude, his soul cracking under the weight of guilt and melancholy. When he emerged from the vegetable shed, another one of those vegan tour buses was just pulling into the driveway and he was forced to stand and greet, grinning insanely, his mind contaminated with the images of Rachlin Roohan and Stalton Preltz twisted together with memories of butcher shop cruelties and commuter-train bathrooms. When Laurette found him that evening, he was hiding behind a machine shed in a patch of pampas grass, staring at clouds that seemed to resemble lovers, entwined at first then sadly drifting apart in tatters and fading to nothingness. She took him by the hand and wiped his cheeks with the sleeve of her coveralls. In signs, she told him she had put their son to bed, though she doubted he would sleep long. She knew, she said, that something terrible had happened, something to do with the past and desire and a hunger all men suffer. She did not judge Tamas, for he had never betrayed her, had brought her nothing but happiness and love. But she remembered how she had found him, bleeding and broken and living with the dog. She only knew now that he must take his son on a journey to the place of sorrows and find the thing they both desired and lose themselves or find themselves. Naturally, she had her preference. But that was for Tamas to decide, and though he might never return his son to innocence, he might find a way to teach him to bear the burden, give him the father-law, and bring him back to her a man before his time. Her words terrified Tamas Preltz, the more so since he didn't really understand them, only that he had to take Stalton away. The next morning they set off for the city, where Tamas hired a private detective to find the Naked Madonna of the Internet, as she had begun to be called. Tamas thought she would be difficult to track, lost somewhere in the electronic ether, but in fact everyone knew where she lived. She had become another roadside attraction, a pop culture icon. Talk shows buzzed with debate, support groups proliferated, preachers thundered from pulpits, public health officials pointed fingers, and politicians wrung their hands. Meanwhile young women all over the country had taken to wearing otter-skin coats and hunting boots. The detective confessed that even he had paid her a visit, and when Tamas looked into his sad eyes, he knew it must be true. He felt a shudder along his spine as though someone had walked over his grave. Something about the detective was familiar to Tamas; it turned out he had once been a prominent Christian conservative politician until he was caught soliciting young men in a train station restroom. "You must have seen me on TV," the detective said. "Say, don't I know you from somewhere?" he asked. But Tamas thought not. The next day he and Stalton drove to the little farming town where he had once worked as a butcher's apprentice. On the outskirts, they found a fusty motel where the *t* in the neon sign no longer shone and creepers grew over the windows. A lone bug zapper sizzled and spat in the twilight, waiting men smoked and jiggled their car keys nervously in their pockets and made anxious telegraphic conversation with their neighbours, hawkers sold french fries and soda, and a local Women's Vigilance Committee had set up a permanent protest. Stalton asked what a "moel" was, and Tamas, feverish with excitement, was unable to answer. Someone came out of the door of number seven, a young man in a neat suit, with a wedding band on his finger. He seemed dazed, unaware of his surroundings, crestfallen, and disappointed. The motel unit door suddenly re-opened and a little black man in voluminous cargo shorts and a vest undershirt scampered out, handing the young man an expensive leather briefcase. The young man looked at the briefcase as though he did not recognize it. Then he walked through the parking lot and disappeared into the twilight. The word "shriven" came unbidden to Tamas Preltz's mind, and he thought how the young man seemed at once ascetic and corrupt, dignified yet shameless, wise and yet powerless to apply that wisdom. It made Tamas shiver to see, some truth there, he thought, no one really wanted to find. He waited two days with his son in that dismal, church-like parking lot, with its pews of waiting acolytes and its mystery of mysteries, holy of holies, watching the men enter and return—always the same expression. Either they are better men or they will kill themselves, he thought on the second day. And then he thought of Stalton, who seemed somehow not there, twisting his hands in his lap, white as fired clay. In vain Tamas tried to hold the little boy's hands, but Stalton would snatch them away with a squeal of impatience. At the end of the second day, weary and dirty, they were bidden through the door by the black attendant, now seen more clearly as elderly, yet wiry, slender, and opaque, blacker than black. The light was dim, the room unkempt, filthy, smelling unspeakably of old rubber and vomit. Takeout food cartons littered the floor. Used condoms hung from the ceiling fixture. The bathroom gas tube flickered and buzzed, casting a sickly green glow. The woman lay drawn up against a stack of pillows at the head of the bed, her coat thrown open, one leg cocked to the side so that her dark triangle splayed open. Dried semen hung like salt or wisps of spiderweb on her thighs and belly. Her ribs all but poked through her skin. Her breasts were tiny and androgynous, all black nipple. She smoked a brown cigarette with a harsh blue smoke that wreathed the room, dug in her ear with a little finger and coughed and smiled enigmatically when she saw the boy and his father, then sucked on the cigarette till ashes fell on her chest and patted the bed in invitation and laughed mirthlessly with a sound like wind in pine trees. She barked something in Swahili, and the African—we know him as Field of

Cows— nudged Stalton forward into the yellow glow of an overhead light. The boy fidgeted, his face pale and pinched, his eyes glassy with fatigue and desire and terror, terror because he did not know what desire was or what he desired, only felt an inchoate and unappeasable need. But he recognized the woman from the Internet site and managed a lugubrious smile, then fainted into a pizza box. Tamas Preltz leaped forward. Rachlin Roohan gasped, staggered to her feet on the bed, and covered herself with the otter-skin coat. "This is the one," she said. "Not him!" she hissed, as the African known as Field of Cows made for Stalton with a short thrusting spear native to his country. "The other," she said. "The one who brought the boy." And simultaneously Tamas Preltz remembered the voice and the face. He remembered the butcher's fat daughter, her nervous laughter, and the dog-girl Megan Strehle barking, "Arf, woof." Now, through Stalton's eyes, he saw the inhuman endlessness of desire, our inability to contain it, the dark tide on which we ride unwitting and unprepared, though even in that moment he wanted to touch Rachlin Roohan, mount her, and bury himself in her body. The universe suddenly seemed alien, death was everywhere, the colours all grey and black and shades of sickly green. Rachlin Roohan's body was skeletal, her face a death's head. He saw himself hung on a hook in a walk-in freezer and then crushed between that woman's emaciated thighs, feeding off her poisonous breasts. One moment he had been happy, with a fat wife, and now the weight of the past, the burden of flesh and the Fall, crushed his heart. He saw his son, innocent and trusting, now trammelled in a web of desire as ineluctable as Fate. He reached for the fallen boy—certain only that coming here had been another in a long line of mistakes leading to some unassimilable ending. But at that moment the African's *assegai* slid between Tamas Preltz's ribs and into his heart. He had only sufficient time to think the word *pity* and touch Stalton's hand as he subsided to the floor. Stalton, recovering from his swoon, recoiled from his father's touch, staring at the Internet whore who, in truth, did not look like much wrapped in her coat. He could not speak, but something came out. It sounded like "Arf, woof."

Some time later, a one-eyed man with a limp descended from a tour bus, followed by a woman Laurette knew but did not know. Stalton caught the sudden tension in his mother's stance; he was washing Brussels sprouts in a diluted food-grade hydrogen peroxide solution under an awning in the open air. He looked just like his father, only younger, somewhat the way Tamas had looked when he was fifteen and worked at Roohan's Butcher Shop. The woman from the bus went rigid at the sight of him, then grasped her friend's hand (his good eye had a desperate cast, a sad glint of corruption that Stalton recognized instantly). Laurette had grown enormous, though her feet and hands remained dainty, her movements graceful and lithe, and her face as friendly and pretty as it had been the day she found Tamas Preltz in Rusty's doghouse. She welcomed the couple and gave them a special tour, including the Tamas Preltz Memorial Industrial Salad Spinner and the Tamas Preltz Ultimate Frisbee Field and the Tamas Preltz Patented Breathable Plastic Bagging Plant. There were photographs of

Tamas Preltz over every doorway: Tamas Preltz as a young man eating his first Brussels sprouts with evident distaste, Tamas Preltz swimming naked in the irrigation pond with Laurette, Tamas Preltz with his famous one-ton pumpkin at the state fair, Tamas Preltz with his beloved children. Megan Strehle grew increasingly agitated as the day wore on. Finally, she could stand it no longer. She broke away from Darter, reached a beringed finger to one of the photographs, and ran the finger around and around the contours of Tamas Preltz's face. She tapped the picture with her nail and said, "I knew him once, long ago. I have looked for him all my life. Sorry, darling," she added, turning to Darter. "It's true." She had tears in her eyes and might have broken down completely except that Laurette Vitapotle embraced her suddenly, crushing her to her oceanic breasts. Megan said, "I am Megan Strehle. He must have spoken of me." And Laurette Vitapotle said, gently, in signs, "Yes, yes, of course. He spoke of you often. He whispered your name in his dreams. I was so jealous." They both knew that this was untrue but became fast friends in that moment.

Meanwhile, Stalton Preltz was not alone. Rachlin Roohan, disguised in a hairnet and dark glasses and co-op coveralls, worked at the washing tubs beside him. She had found her way to the farm to beg forgiveness, to try to make amends for all the trouble she had caused. The day she arrived, Laurette Vitapotle and Rachlin Roohan secluded themselves in a sorting shed. The murmur of their secret colloquy emanated from the shed until nightfall and then through the night. No one dared go near. Once, there was a shriek and a low moan—whether it was Laurette's voice or Rachlin's, no one could tell. More than once there came the bubbling sound of crying, another time there was laughter, then more laughter near the end. In the morning, the two women emerged hand in hand, one hugely obese, a primordial Venus, the other skeletal, both in tears. Rachlin Roohan found a bed in the field-hand barracks. And neither woman ever talked about that night except once Laurette said she had asked Rachlin if she had gotten what she wanted. And Rachlin Roohan had said no, she had never known what she wanted, and what she thought she wanted had only been a screen of error. But from the moment of her arrival, Stalton Preltz's melancholy had begun to lift, as though seeing the real Rachlin Roohan dressed in ordinary clothes (aside from the hairnet and dark glasses), and not the Internet fantasy, somehow relieved his obsessions. One day, much later, he met a girl his own age and they fell in love and were married. Once in a while she would dress up in an otter-skin coat and hunting boots and their lovemaking would be tinged with sadness, though perhaps this is so of all love.

Field of Cows was arrested for Tamas Preltz's murder, which he confessed to unreservedly. Some alert police officer noticed that his passport had expired, and he was declared an Enemy Combatant and waterboarded until he confessed again. He was put on a black flight to an undisclosed East European country for further questioning, where, under torture, he confessed yet again. Several intelligence agencies were determined to break him and find the truth, but he stuck to his story: he and he alone had killed Tamas Preltz with a Masai lion spear at a remote motel somewhere in America.

One night, in an attempt to end it all, Field of Cows jumped from his turret cell window over a cliff and into a raging river at the bottom of a gorge. He was found more than half dead the next day by a former Romanian state garlic farmer named Nicola Romanescu, nursed back to health, and he lives there now, tending Nicola's crops, an embittered and rancorous old man whom no one can understand, for which reason he is considered mystical and wise by the locals. An investigation into his mysterious crimes and disappearance is ongoing on four continents and is considered a matter of national security in several world capitals.

When the tour bus left, Megan Strehle and her companion Darter stayed on. They liked the place. Some feeling remained of the joyous lovemaking, and there was a sense of shared humanity, something straight to the heart that came from having a connection with the past that was at once harsh and cruel and exciting. All the survivors remembered Tamas Preltz fondly. No one, they felt, was to blame for the disconcerting vagaries of life. All their hearts were good and true, they thought. Soon a younger generation began to pair off (as has been indicated above) and sounds of love, peals of laughter, and whispers like the sound of wind in pine trees filled the summer nights anew.

Uncle Boris Up in a Tree

The photo was taken just before all hell broke loose. Uncle Boris, always the clown, perches on a tree branch above the family group, making a mockery of the occasion. Jannik, the wastrel, smiles inscrutably. Bjorn, the straight arrow, looks like a man with all the troubles of the world on his shoulders, but he works in a bank in town and can afford a gold watch and fob. His eyes are closed. Gurn, the insane one, his mouth twisted from a horse kick, seems merely confused, innocent, and anxious. Lisel, the compulsive smoker and Bible reader, has momentarily suppressed her persistent and fatal cough. The three young ones huddle with Ma and Pa: Trig, later executed for murder, only six in the photo and dressed like a girl; Grete, who became a great lover; and little Nikolai, the math genius, eight months old. Bjorn's wife Olga, plain as a pine plank but seething with desire, leans against the tree trunk next to Jannik. Aunt Doreen, flighty, excitable, and dim, stares at the camera warily. Daphne, the family slut, has her hands in her skirt pockets and her head tilted to one side.

*

It begins like this: a family dinner, alfresco despite the lateness of the year, just after the turnips were in and the hog slaughtered. Bjorn walks behind the barn to pee and discovers his wife Olga in a passionate embrace with Jannik, the wastrel. At first, the couple remain unaware of Bjorn's presence. They whisper sweet, desperate nothings in each other's ears. "Oh, my little potato bug!" "Oh, you bad boy, you bad, bad boy, oh!" Bjorn knows that Jannik sleeps with girls in town. He's even discussed with Olga how Jannik seduced one of the bank tellers. Jannik is drunk half the time. He borrows money from his parents to spend at the dance halls and buy presents for his girls. Bjorn sees nothing charming in him. When they were boys, Bjorn was forever finishing the fights Jannik provoked. The scene behind the barn repulses Bjorn. He doesn't want to be the straight arrow any more. Suddenly, he doesn't remember why he married Olga. They have been trying to have a baby for three years, long nights of sweaty labour sawing away under the goose feather quilt. She nags at him to ask Herr Grimmig for a raise. She is always accusing him of sleeping with the tellers at the bank. She calls the teller pool his private harem. Now she sighs and squeals, trembling in Jannik's embrace; Jannik thrusts himself against her and fumbles with her skirts. The white flesh of her doughy thighs flashes in the October sunlight. Seeing her flesh, Bjorn feels an unaccustomed throb of desire. He should object, but there is nothing he can say now that will make this scene better. Yet he cannot tear himself away. Then Olga, with a shriek, notices him at the corner of the barn. Their eyes meet. It breaks the spell. Bjorn claps his hat on his head and turns on his heel, thinking only of escape, relieved almost, turgid with desire. Suddenly, time, which had seemed forever stalled in a state of minute reiterations of itself, begins to flow again. He feels the current under his elbows, tugging him along. Olga frantically pushes Jannik away. Bjorn glimpses drab nether hair, petticoats, and the tip of Jannik's erect penis like a small purple heart. Olga catches up with him at the gate. "That didn't mean anything," she says. "I had too much potato vodka. Jannik made me. I was confused." Bjorn towers over her. He can't think of anything to say. It seems like a speech from some other drama, staged long ago. Her breath smells like red onions and garlic, an odour he associates with love. "Anyway, I'm pregnant," she says. Bjorn's shoulders sag. Suddenly, the doors of his cage clang shut again. The doors are called duty and responsibility. The entire family is watching from the blankets spread on the lawn amid the squirts of goose shit and pats of cow dung. Chickens, geese, and eight-week-old shoats wander from plate to plate looking for leftovers. "Enough," says Bjorn, allowing himself to be led back to the festivities. Jannik's shirt-tail hangs out. He throws his head back and guffaws at something Pa says. There is a war in Bjorn's head. Briefly he becomes a philosopher. He thinks, What does it mean to be alive? How should one behave? He gazes up at the sky, cold and numbingly blue. Trig, always the sensitive one, bursts into tears. Uncle Boris is climbing the tree again, trying to make everyone laugh. Bjorn catches up a bottle of potato vodka from the blanket and whirls away. He has the air of a man who is never coming back. Two of the shoats start to drag baby Nikolai toward the bushes. Daphne, the slut, laughing, rescues him and clutches him to her breasts. Olga cries, "If it's a boy, we'll name him Bjorn."

In the days that follow, Pa remembers that Bjorn's bank owns the farm. He has been borrowing money and losing it for years. Pigs and turnips never seemed to catch on. He tried asparagus once, but the pigs ate the asparagus. Bjorn convinced him to modernize by buying a computer for his accounts. He keeps a list of the pigs, their birthdates, and their weights. Every weekend, he catches the pigs, weighs them, and enters the new weights on a spreadsheet called Pigs. Bjorn didn't tell him how this was going to make money or pay off the loan. In another file he keeps a list of his children, their birthdates, and their weights. He doesn't know what the older children weigh any more. In yet another file he keeps track of the number of people living in his house and how many square feet each person occupies. And in a fourth file he notes everything each person eats and how much he would charge if he were operating his family as a business. It gives him some satisfaction to know that if he did charge room and board, he could have paid off the bank loan years before. Pa moves into the barn to get away from his children, who are not working out the way he had expected. He catches the piglets and weighs them and plays solitaire on the computer. He senses a drift in the life of things, a massive inconsequentiality. He thinks of the mole on Ma's left breast, shaped like a rabbit and sprouting three dark hairs she strokes and flattens during her morning reveries. He remembers that when he was a boy, he wanted to be a painter. He didn't even know what a painter was. Now he drags out tins of leftover house paint, cleans his brushes, and begins to slap out garish murals on the inside walls of the barn. He tries to paint the pigs, but they run around and rub against each other and smudge the paint. Pa has never felt as happy as he does now, painting his vast picture. Since they have nothing else to do, the children sit in the barn and watch and offer helpful criticism. At first Pa doesn't mind, but soon they begin to tell him secrets. They confess their lies, their sins, and their darkest desires. Jannik pats a pig painted to look like a dachshund and says that he doesn't love Olga but wants to propose to the bank teller instead. He needs money to buy her a make-up present. Daphne confesses that she cannot keep her legs closed, that she wanders into town without any underdrawers beneath her skirt and offers herself to strangers. She is happiest of the children, Pa notices. Trig chases a piglet with a pitchfork with murderous intent, but his skirts tangle in his short, ungainly legs, and the piglets are, so far, too quick for him. Next to Bjorn, Trig seems the least happy. Bjorn has gone back to work in the bank. Days, Jannik sneaks into town and sleeps with Olga. Olga slaps the walls when she comes and makes wild and indiscreet noises as she labours under his thighs. She tells Jannik she has never felt so alive, so wonderful. "You make me feel beautiful," she says. The words chill him. He can hardly bear to look at her face. Every time they sleep together, he is racked with guilt toward his brother. Evenings, Olga sets a plate of peas and radishes for Bjorn and sips potato vodka and tells him what an oaf, what a failure he is. She screams at him about his harem of secretaries and claims to smell sex and eau de cologne on his clothes. Sometimes she just leaves the plate of peas and radishes and drives back to the farm and sits giggling in the loft with Daphne, comparing their lovers. Boris entertains everyone by pretending that his job is to move the manure pile. He actually does move the manure pile every day, from behind the barn to the front yard or the potato field or the coal cellar, and then again the next day. Every morning, Jannik and Daphne take turns telling him to move the manure pile, and Boris throws his head back and laughs till tears roll down his cheeks, and then he fetches a shovel and wheelbarrow and moves the manure pile.

Gurn falls into a depression, only no one notices because he is already silent and crazy. His scarred lips twist in unspeakable agonies. He leaves notes tacked to the refrigerator door with magnets in the shape of pigs. "Why does the manure pile keep moving?" he wonders. "Why does Bjorn live in town with that ugly woman?" The slightest change in routine Gurn takes as a personal assault. He feels constantly victimized by Fate, a plaything of the gods. "The Universe is an inexplicable mystery," he writes. He thinks, What does it mean to be alive? How should one behave? Without telling anyone, he sends away for literature about assisted suicide. Eventually he will hang himself from the branch where Uncle Boris sat for the photograph, but not in this story. Nights, while her father is sleeping, Daphne sneaks into the barn and uses his computer to sign onto an Internet dating site where she posts naked photographs of herself taken in the bathroom mirror. She likes to read *Jane Eyre* in a hammock strung between two cedars in the backyard. She wants to find an old blind man like Rochester whom she can love and care for. "I will be your eyes," she whispers to herself. "I will be your eyes," she whispers to every man she sleeps with. At heart she is a true romantic. She is a true romantic who likes sex. Grete overhears her sister's whispers. "I will be your eyes." She picks up the discarded book and begins to read. Lisel chain-smokes hand-rolled cigarettes in the hayloft, reading her Bible by a candle in a bronze holder. In a notebook she keeps a list of people God smites for no good reason. Aunt Doreen watches Pa paint another shoat to look like a Dalmatian, only red with green spots. She opines that she is probably a lesbian. She tells her brother that Amy Rastinhad touched her breasts when she was thirteen and she has been in love with Amy ever since, though Amy moved away to a big city in the East and disappeared from her life. She wishes they had made love, because now she is forty-two and it doesn't look as if she'll ever make love to anyone and it makes her flighty and nervous. "I am not as empty-headed as I seem, only empty-hearted," she says, looking vague and empty-headed, fretting her hair with her fingers, picking at split ends and crossing her eyes. Pa puts the finishing dab of paint on the pig and unties its legs just as Trig makes a lunge with the fork. Pa wishes they would stop telling him their secrets. He has enough trouble just feeding them all and keeping them in underdrawers and socks. His family is nothing but a cesspit of passion, delusion, self-pity, egomania, and borderline personality disorder. It bothers him that his children seem so driven, that they act out of boredom or compulsion, that despite their confessions, their real motives and inspirations remain secret and hidden, even from themselves. Nights, Ma trips out to the barn in her nightie and they make love on a paint-spattered drop cloth thrown over bales of hay. Paint smudges her cheeks and thighs, hay tickles their noses, he kisses her rabbit mole, she sneezes, makes little farts, heaves her heavy thighs, and moans. Prior to this they had not spoken in five years and Pa had slept on a hard bench in the hallway on a pile of coats. But something has changed, as if the vast complex machinery of the cosmos has shifted slightly—mysteriously and secretly. Now they laugh and shout and slap each other's backsides pink, and Pa rubs his nose in Ma's capacious belly.

Like Gurn, the country is in a depression, much like every other country in the world. The bottom has fallen out of the real estate market. Herr Grimmig, the bank manager, sends Bjorn out to repossess properties every day. The first day, a bankrupt computer repairman threatens to slit his children's throats, bludgeon his wife to death, and then kill himself. He breaks down in tears, muttering, "I don't know what to do. My teeth hurt. There's no money." Bjorn tries to get Herr Grimmig to renegotiate the loan. "We should go broke?" says Herr Grimmig. "He brought this failure on himself. The marketplace is the new God." Herr Grimmig is an ascetic sixty-year-old with a tennis-player tan and a languid graciousness that makes even the worst news sound unexceptional and even mildly pleasant. A week later, the bankrupt computer repairman slaughters his children and wife and burns the house down over their bodies, then gives himself up to the police. Neighbours tell reporters he was a quiet family man and they would never have suspected he was a homicidal maniac, though in their hearts, they remember him as a brooding, violent man obsessed with keeping his front yard free of weeds and threatening to shoot children who cut across on their way to school. (Back at the farm, young Trig cuts out the newspaper article with his snub-nosed preschool scissors.) Bjorn begins spending his days at a roadhouse called The Wingless Phalarope. Instead of serving papers on low-life homeowners, he sits at a white table under an awning and drinks peppermint schnapps in tall shot glasses with little etched bird patterns. In fact he is supposed to serve papers on Tamara Winzcheslon, owner of The Wingless Phalarope, but he cannot bear to make another person unhappy. So he drinks with her instead and commiserates about her dead husband, who was lost at sea when environmentalist protesters sank his fishing boat. "What were they protesting?" he asks. Tamara shrugs. "He was minding his own business—the usual crime." While Tamara is pouring drinks for other customers, Bjorn concocts elaborate schemes to conceal his inability to serve papers on poor people. He creates dummy corporations and offshore holding companies and bizarre oscillating land swaps and uses the paper profits to finance complex futures plays in pork bellies and turnips. Reading the daily spreadsheets over his shoulder, Tamara pats him on the head and kisses his bald spot. "Who owns my sweet little taverna this morning?" she asks. Herr Grimmig decides to promote Bjorn. Somehow the paper profits turn into real profits. The glowing screen of Bjorn's computer makes no distinction. Bjorn buys a lemon-yellow Land Rover on eBay. Olga clasps her pregnant belly and squeals with delight. When Jannik, the wastrel, comes by the next day, he finds the door locked. But Olga calls him back from the bus stop at the corner and invites him in one last time, overcome with the tragedy of his bitter disappointment. She thinks, I hate myself. How should one behave? What does it really mean to be alive? She doesn't understand why she is so bitter toward Bjorn, the innocent in all this. Nights, she waits anxiously for the sound of his feet on the doorstep. But then he greets her with a look of wariness. His wary eyes inquire, What is she going to do next? And she explodes with rage. Every hateful thing she says, and she is very good at inventing them—she could win the Nobel Prize for Hateful Things Shouted at a Husband—seems right and true in the moment. Like everyone else, she wants a moment of true feeling. But panic and rage come easier.

"You'll end up in jail," says Pa, when Bjorn drives up in the lemon-yellow Land Rover and confesses his fraudulent speculations. "Why tell me about this?" he adds. Bjorn waves a sheaf of papers in Pa's face. "I am supposed to repossess the farm today," he says. He peers up at Pa's barn-wall mural, sucking in his breath in surprise. The painting stretches past the roof beams onto the peaked ceiling where there is barely any light, a vast array of exuberant life panels, a narrative of the family history complete with the names and slaughter weights of generations of pigs. At the beginning Ma and Pa cavort naked around the tree in the front yard, Adam and Eve, only Ma is a tight-bodied, slender-hipped adolescent Venus with a mischievous look and Pa is a golden-haired hero. Uncle Boris is up in the tree in a nightcap. Babies and turnips sprout in the fields. A lone grey phalarope perches atop a sow rooting among the turnips. Geese and chickens pick daintily at the manure pile. In panel after panel the children grow taller, more babies appear. The farm looks like a jungle, like a primeval garden. Ma and Pa scamper hand in hand amongst the trees. To Bjorn it seems indecent, though strangely exciting. Bjorn confesses to Pa that he has begun writing poetry in his afternoons at The Wingless Phalarope, in between cellphone calls with developers and Internet billionaires. Herr Grimmig drives to The Wingless Phalarope to consult, not wishing to interrupt Bjorn's precious work schedule. He depends on Bjorn to help him with all his bank decisions. Tamara Winzcheslon serves Bjorn peppermint schnapps and coffee and sometimes sits across the table from him with her chin on her hand, longing for him. But Bjorn is a faithful husband. In fact he can be a bit of a bore on the subject. And so Tamara is sleeping with Joran Boze, the dishwasher, to make Bjorn jealous and to have some fun. Nights, Bjorn sleeps next to Olga, who tosses and sighs, sweating with desire and frustration in the stale sheets. When they try to make love, it is all tedium and effort. She accuses him of having sex with Tamara Winzcheslon. Her belly expands, she looks like a snake that has swallowed a football. When he puts his ear down there, Bjorn can hear the heartbeat. He says to Pa, "I don't understand what life is about. All I can think of is the possibility that I will get brain cancer and die horribly before I have a chance to be happy." Pa says, "Come and have dinner. Trig killed one of the shoats. He's a handy little butcher, you know. At least one of my sons will have a trade." To Bjorn, his father looks half dead from care. The multicoloured pigs keep warily to the shadows, crowding together in protective groups. Pa and Bjorn smell smoke and climb into the loft, where they find Lisel asleep beside her overturned candle. They put out the fire with their coats.

Jannik, the wastrel, borrows money from Ma to buy the teller a gold necklace with a tiny seabird charm attached. The teller's name is Agnes Botgaard, and she is secretly in love with Herr Grimmig. But she accepts the necklace and pretends to like Jannik because Herr Grimmig won't pay any attention to her and Jannik's brother might soon own the bank. Jannik suspects something is up because the sex isn't so good. He thinks illicit sex is the best; he likes the first weeks of a new affair when all sorts of hanky-panky seem possible. He craves that abandonment in pleasure. Now he wishes he had not bought the necklace, wishes he had used the money to gamble instead. Suddenly he feels obligated to Agnes Botgaard. He has the strange thought that he must somehow do right by her. He has never felt this way. She tells him it's okay, he doesn't have to do right by her. It can be a one-night stand. He wonders what to do next. He thinks, How should one behave? What does it mean to be alive? Like many people in that economically and spiritually repressed land, Jannik has few options and no fun except for illicit sex and gambling. He notices that in the present age people are turning to art and sex to pass the time. His father's barn murals are beginning to attract attention. Much to Pa's disgust, his barn is now included on local vacation bus tours, along with the desalinization plant, the cement factory, the abandoned canal lock, the salt marsh, and the earthen dikes where multicoloured cows graze placidly. Daphne poses naked for local art groups that have sprung up like mushrooms in the cultural darkness. The town newspaper's columns are taken up with virulent aesthetic disputes between the right-wing realists, the left-wing avant-garde, and the irritatingly articulate postmoderns, despised by all. Jannik notices that the newspaper is also publishing his brother's poems, pages of them, and photos of his new house in the gated community going up along the salt marsh nesting grounds. Bjorn has a swimming pool and a personal gymnasium, and there are photos of Olga, big as a barn, reading celebrity magazines in a bikini. The shoats should be full-grown by now, but many have mysteriously disappeared. Boris finds caches of bones when he moves the manure pile. He is running out of new places to move the manure pile. The joke is getting old. His face is haggard and drawn. Around the neighbourhood, small pets are also disappearing. Daphne is more popular than ever, now that nude paintings of her adorn gallery walls across the country. An elderly gent with a white cane comes calling, asking for Grete, and the elderly man and the girl walk down the laneway to the dikes and the salt marsh, their heads bending together in animated conversation, her hand lightly touching his forearm as she guides him through gates and over stiles. Though he can't see, she points out the various sights to him. In the distance she can see Bjorn's new house, rising like a palace beyond the new yacht club. Nikolai cannot speak yet but solves intricate math problems with a toy abacus. Gurn tests slip-knots on rope samples from the hardware store in town. He has never seemed happier. His twisted mouth knots up in a grimace, impossible to read. Lisel begins to study ancient Greek and Hebrew through an online university in Arizona. Aunt Doreen writes a letter to Amy Rastinhad, now Mrs. Artemis Hagedoorn. One day a taxi, spewing oily smoke from its exhaust, stops at the gate. A tall, slim, sad-looking woman with a large flowery hat steps out and gazes up at Uncle Boris, sitting in the tree. Aunt Doreen totters along the dirt path to the gate and Uncle Boris watches the two women embrace, a long look of relief on their faces. Then Aunt Doreen takes one of the woman's bags and guides her toward the house.

Olga makes love with Gurn in the hayloft. This is during Christmas dinner when, once again, the whole family celebrates together and Ma cooks the usual roast pig and turnip dumplings. It's a surprise to everyone, including Olga and Gurn. Bjorn goes to the front stoop for a smoke and hears her cries of ecstasy and discovers Gurn with his trousers at his ankles, thrusting between Olga's legs from behind (on account of her ponderous belly), his twisted mouth twisted into a fantastic grin of delight, the loft floor shaking beneath them, the brilliant greens and golds and pinks of Pa's epic painting climbing the walls like smoke, like dream maps. Olga had not intended this, but something about Gurn's scars had lately begun to obsess her. She wondered what it would be like to kiss those awful lips, wondered if poor Gurn had ever made love, wondered at the degradation of submitting herself to his disfigurement. After a couple of tumblers of potato vodka, she lost all inhibition. Instead of trying to explain this to Bjorn, she merely spreads her legs in a languid motion and allows him a better view of Gurn's veined erection sliding into her thatched vulva. Her underdrawers bag around one ankle. Her smock rucks up at her throat, revealing her vast fertile belly and distended breasts with nipples like dinner plates. She imagines herself a picture of filth and female satisfaction, an ancient oriental princess being serviced by a slave on a couch of damask and leopard pelt. But Bjorn barely notices her after he spies a grown pig, painted like the map of the world, peeking warily from a niche in the hay bales. The pig's eyes meet Bjorn's eyes with a look of terror and wisdom, a fatalistic look that makes Bjorn suddenly ashamed. Gurn comes with a shout of dismay. Olga shuts her eyes and seems to settle into herself, the image of saintly depravity. Bjorn envies the pig and Olga and even Gurn for their animal natures, for their ability to abandon decorum and act out of avarice and desire, just as he envies Pa for his ability to live in a barn and irresponsibly paint pictures while farm and family go to ruin.

Bjorn, the straight arrow, has a gold watch and fob, symbols of rectitude, his mastery of time, like a lock on his soul. Rather than feeling the usual tumescent jealousy at the sight of Olga's amorous paroxysms, Bjorn now senses a vast pity in his heart. He understands that Olga is hungry for love, that she feels trapped in her marriage, in her plainness, in her pregnancy, all those forms of living that have nothing to do with the person she knows herself to be, that she longs for the thrill of something real, a strange man's touch, beyond reason or obligation, his breath on the nape of her neck, his hardness probing her most intimate parts. He also understands that Olga understands that he understands. Gurn, who understands nothing, thinks, Why does she love strangers and not the man she loves? In the dining room, Pa and Ma pet and flirt shamelessly. Pa tweaks Ma's nipples through her dress with his paint-smeared hands. Jannik, the wastrel, lowers a proprietary arm over Agnes Botgaard's shoulder. He announces their impending marriage; he doesn't want to marry her but has vowed to live a better life after betraying Bjorn so egregiously with his pregnant wife. (Actually, the baby is Jannik's, though no one except Olga will ever know this.) Jannik is taking accounting courses and has applied for a position in the bank. He published a poem in the town newspaper. Out of guilt, he wants to become his brother, though every move in that direction makes him feel as if he is lowering himself into a grave. Agnes looks radiantly happy, although this is only because her engagement to Jannik has provoked Herr Grimmig's jealousy and he has invited her for a New Year's Eve punch at The Wingless Phalarope. Aunt Doreen sits in a corner sipping thimbles of potato vodka with her lover, their hands clasped, their thighs pressed together in a line to their knees, their faces hovering so near that they breathe each other's breath. Since Amy Rastinhad arrived, no one has heard either woman speak a word, but they are inseparable and spend most of their time behind the locked bedroom door. When Bjorn, Gurn, and Olga return from the barn, young Trig slips out the back and, in the distance, they hear the death shriek of a sow. This is a week after Nikolai disappeared, when the whole family went into a hysterical panic until the boy was discovered hiding in a neighbour's doghouse with the last of the shoats. Hearing the pig's dying cry and imagining the tide of clotting blood dripping through the haymow planks, Bjorn knows that he is unequal to the task of being a poet, that reality is too real for him ever to capture it in a rhyming couplet, that there is too much violence, drama, and wayward passion to fit into a sonnet, that form deforms the truth just as decorum deforms personality. Every step he takes, Bjorn feels as if he is lowering himself into a grave. To everyone's delight, Uncle Boris capers about, uttering nonsense rhymes, dressed in Bavarian hunting costume. He tells them he has taken the day off and will not be moving the manure pile. He knocks over the Christmas fir, trying to climb into its higher branches.

Bjorn wins a national prize for his poetry. He is lauded in the media as "the banker poet." Bjorn vows never to write another poem and, under the pseudonym Alonzo Cutlip, publishes a critique condemning himself as a conventional, sentimental, bland hack (which, as a poet, he is). "What does it say of the poem," he asks, "if it is praised in the gutter press, finds favour with the usual editors, and is read with pleasure by the illiterate masses? One must aim to write the unreadable poem!" Olga delivers a baby boy, the very image of Jannik right down to the widow's peak twisted into a spit curl at the top of his forehead. He has a flirtatious (wastrel) look from the start. They call him Bjorn 2 or Little Bjorn. Agnes Botgaard breaks off her engagement to Jannik after her New Year's Eve tryst with Herr Grimmig. Jannik is crushed, his heart is broken. He drops in at The Wingless Phalarope, drowns his sorrows in nineteen glasses of Pilsner with peppermint schnapps depth charges, kisses Tamara Winzcheslon under the mistletoe in front of her lover Joran Boze for half an hour (sets fire to her lonely heart), then visits his favourite casino, The Abyss, and wins a small fortune at blackjack. He forgets to cash in his chips, but an alert floor manager presses a bag of zlotys into his hands. The stock market slumps, consumer confidence turns into suspicion and doubt. Pa becomes the leader of a booming art movement called the Even More Eccentric Rural Primitives, made up mostly of retired schoolteachers, unemployed factory workers, and young college graduates who can't find jobs, all painting rapturous mythic murals on the walls of their apartments in imitation of the Master. Famous art auction houses offer to sell Pa's barn to the highest bidder. In the villages and suburbs nearby, children begin to disappear with alarming frequency. Uncle Boris strolls up and down the front walk with his hands in his pockets, unable to think of anything better to do now that there are no more pigs and the manure pile has been replaced with recycling bins. Aunt Doreen whispers to Pa that her relationship with Amy Rastinhad is dwindling. She dreams, at night, of naked men, admits to Pa that perhaps she is only in love with what she cannot have. One day, a taxi pulls up at the gate, and Aunt Doreen hands Amy Rastinhad's bag to the driver, and the tall, elegant woman in the flowered hat rolls away in a cloud of dust, a pink monogrammed hanky waving bravely at the taxi window. Daphne elopes with an orchestra — not a member of the orchestra, but the entire string and reed sections. No one tells Pa, which, for him, is a relief. Grete, much too young for romance, continues to receive the blind, elderly man, whose name is Mr. Quimby. Someone hears her say, "I will be your eyes." (When she says the words, they are full of gentle innocence and selflessness, in contrast to Daphne, for whom the words are an unconscious tactic in a game of erotic conquest.) She reads to him in the front parlour where no one ever goes except during those periodic joyous family get-togethers. Sometimes she leads him through the barn, stopping before the great, soaring, glittering panels to describe the colours and stories. Mr. Quimby says to Pa, "These are wonderful pictures. I can tell by the smell of the paint." Gurn cheerfully writes and rewrites his will. He puts his affairs in order, and then he puts them in a different order. Bjorn tries to love little Bjorn 2 but can't. He resigns himself to an empty facade of dutiful parenting just as the sensitive Bjorn 2, realizing what is what, resigns himself to a joyless imitation of a childhood. Soon Bjorn 2 and Bjorn begin to resemble one another, they wear the same stern, blank expression in the face of life's furious injustice. Without the baby inside her, Olga looks like a collapsed balloon. She feels even less attractive. At night she lies next to Bjorn in an agony of frustration and desire, but his touch makes her skin crawl, not the touch she desires. She accuses Bjorn of being a homosexual because he doesn't make love to her. She accuses him of sleeping with Herr Grimmig. She recites whole litanies of his failings and betrayals. For a man so infuriatingly polite, faithful, dutiful, earnest, and socially conscious, Bjorn has a lot to answer for. Lisel is diagnosed with emphysema and walks around with her cigarettes, books, and an oxygen tank like a literate deep-sea diver dragging her aqualung on a cart. To everyone's amazement, she abandons her close reading of the Apocrypha in Aramaic and begins studying translations of ancient Sanskrit erotic texts. She confesses to Pa that she has been secretly dating an unemployed dishwasher named Joran Boze whom she met in the town library where he was trying to find a job on the Internet. Nights, Lisel and Joran meet at The Wingless Phalarope, where she takes off her oxygen mask so they can kiss and sip peppermint schnapps. As often as not, they will find Bjorn working over the bank's balance sheets, also sipping peppermint schnapps (in those distinctive tall shot glasses with the strange seabird design), absent-mindedly dandling Bjorn 2 on his knee. In the kitchen, Tamara Winzcheslon and Jannik, the wastrel, will be throwing plates at each other, squabbling about his wastrel ways, after which they rush upstairs and make love with wild abandon. At some point, Uncle Boris breaks an arm falling out of the tree.

*

Bjorn dreams that Pulch, the cobbler, accosts him in the street with a shout. "Your shoes are ready!" Pulch holds out a pair of strangely shaped workboots with hobnails and laces up to the ankles. But the boots are only half complete, with toe tips missing and gaping open like a cross-section. Bjorn knows somehow that these are miner's boots. He needs them to go underground. At the pithead, there is a bustling confusion of smoke, flame, and milling crowds. An awesome black tower of girders and cables rises above, supporting the machinery of the mine lift, a mighty gate to nowhere. Bjorn descends in a cage filled with grim soot-faced men, women, even children, also dogs, horses and pigs, all with lamps, helmets and shovels. Their faces are sombre and frightened as the lift drops down and down, faster and faster, and the rank walls of the mine shaft disappear and are replaced with an inky blackness. The mine shaft is inexpressibly cold. Bjorn's face aches with the wind of the cage's falling. In the distance now, he sees stars, whole constellations and galaxies he doesn't recognize. Still the lift descends. A beautiful woman (who somehow reminds him of Olga) touches his cheek with a finger and whispers, "You're going home. Don't you know?"

The story ends with a wedding. One evening Jannik catches Tamara Winzcheslon's eye as she polishes bird glasses behind the gleaming phalarope-shaped beer spigots—a little girl's pout, vulnerable dip of her irises, look of love. The curve of her belly just inside her pelvic crest is the most beautiful thing

Jannik has ever seen in his life. Like all dead fishermen's wives, she is a sexual renegade between the sheets simply because she already knows how things will end. Is it love he feels? Jannik is dazed by the sublime horror and mystery of the question. And he cannot answer it. But, as a lifelong wastrel, he is equally incapable of denying the instinct that tells him marriage to a woman who owns a profitable bar is a prudent option. It will be neither the first nor the last time a human being does the right thing for the wrong reason. The wedding is supposed to take place under a tent in the front yard at the farm. But the weather is so promising that Pa orders the tent taken down as an aesthetic monstrosity that obstructs his view. Then a fog rolls in off the salt marsh, and a gentle rain begins to fall. Music is provided by an itinerant klezmer band called Prophets in the Wilderness (friends of Daphne). The local justice of the peace officiates (a man named Frank Mahovlich who has narrow shoulders, a pot-belly, bad breath, a wandering eye, a moth-eaten tailcoat, and is otherwise extraneous to the story—you can just assume he has his own plot problems). Two couples stand up before Frank Mahovlich: Lisel and Joran Boze and Jannik and Tamara Winzcheslon. Everyone agrees the occasion is sweet and holy. The young women (Tamara, actually, not so young) wear the usual white meringues that make them look awkward, overweight, embarrassed, and brazen all at once (Lisel somewhat encumbered as well with her breathing apparatus). The grooms wear identical too-tight dinner jackets and canary-yellow cummerbunds (Pa picked the colours); freshly shaved and glistening, they look, to Bjorn, like penises tied with bows. Muttering to himself,

Uncle Boris rehearses dirty jokes for his speech, picking his way nervously amid goose squirts and cow pats. A fresh batch of shoats gathers beneath the banquet table (Pa buys them for companionship; they don't seem to last long). A general atmosphere of bashful lustiness, uncertainty, mystery, solemnity, terror, and misplaced hope pervades the drizzly scene. At the last moment, in an access of joy (Ma had just bent over to taste the turnip salad and he caught a glimpse of the rabbit mole on her breast), Pa falls to his knees and proposes that they marry again. Ma squeals and exclaims that it's the best proposal she's ever had, and she accepts.

Bjorn, misty-eyed from the mist, can't help but smile. For no reason, he gives Olga a little poke in her deflated belly. She glances up at him irritably. Bjorn is thinking about Bjorn 2, how they have become inseparable, united, apparently, by their inability to love one another. No one has ever understood Bjorn as well as Bjorn 2. With a jolt, a sudden ache like a gas pain, Bjorn realizes that maybe this is love. Olga sees that he is smiling and thinks, Oh, Bjorn is being idiotically sentimental or just idiotic. But he keeps smiling, and there is something strange in his eyes, an expression that is at once sad, distant, weighing, thinking, alive. Olga feels a pang of compassion. It occurs to her that Bjorn can see his death coming toward him. Bjorn thinks: The universe is a complete mystery to me. How should one behave? What does it mean to be a human being? All my life I have seen my death coming toward me. Then he says an astonishing thing, words that break the form, a blind leap. He says, "We should get married too." Olga says, "What?" Waspish, irritable, impatient, surprised, puzzled, bitter. Bjorn says, "We should get married again. I think I haven't loved you enough. I married you the first time out of pity because you were the last of the ugly Klapp girls and without a dowry. Don't mistake me—I thought that was love at the time, but now I see it differently." He keeps smiling that inane smile. He feels suddenly free. All the world's cares, responsibilities, and claims seem to drop away. He understands that he is giving up on himself, and that, paradoxically, he has never felt more like himself. He feels like a corpse climbing out of a grave. Olga takes a breath and thinks, Perhaps I have been holding my breath these ten years. There is a trace of a smile on her lips. She says, "I am plain as a pine plank." "Whoever said such a thing?" says Bjorn. "The author," says Olga. "Besides, it's true." She says, "I was always afraid you'd never like me, that you'd run away." "It doesn't matter," says Bjorn, a bit irritated about the author. "I love you now." Olga asks, shyly, tentatively, still with the faint wisp of a smile breaking on her thin lips, "Even after all the bad things I have done?" "Because of everything you have done," Bjorn says. "They are signs of life," he says. "I want to start again," he says. There is another of those pregnant silences. Suddenly, Bjorn and Olga realize everyone is watching. No one has seen Bjorn and Olga hold a remotely friendly conversation in years. Now they are clasping hands, shyly offering themselves to Mahovlich's ritual mumbling.

Four couples get married under the tree, a mass expression of baseless, irrational optimism. Uncle Boris watches the ceremony from his perch on the branch. He forgets his speech.

He can't get his new safety harness undone, so he ends up sleeping in the tree till morning, much fretted by mosquitoes. And, truth be told, except for the catering assistant found with a pitchfork in her throat behind the barn after the reception, everyone lives happily ever after. For a while.

Savage Love

On Tuesday, Ona Frame went to see his friend Shelby to discuss the Betsy Edger affair, which had erupted in the spring just when he was getting over what they both referred to as the "Regrettable Incident" involving the drug-addicted, emotionally intense but self-centred former small-time movie actress with the luminous face, who had briefly enticed Ona and Shelby into an insanely competitive if not vicious romantic triangle that threatened the foundations of their friendship.

Ona Frame had initially regarded Betsy Edger, a would-be author and part-time book-stacker at the local public library, as a transitional love object, someone whose tranquil, no-affect disposition promised little drama and fewer demands and also seemed, prudently enough, the antithesis of Shelby's type (dramatic, histrionic, large-breasted blondes with unfinished doctorates and fetishistic erotic tendencies). But then Shelby fell harder than ever for Betsy Edger, and the same situation had developed as before.

Quiet, calm, immature, undemanding, monosyllabic, untalented, plain, auburn-haired Betsy Edger had turned sexually voracious overnight, it seemed, and would leave Ona's narrow bed in the moonlight, dress quickly and carelessly in the clothes she had just slipped out of, sometimes leaving a soiled intimate article apparently by accident, and rush, with neither apology nor excuse, across town to Shelby's palatial, adults-only condominium with the hot-tub-and-pool combo and the wet bar beside his computer workstation where he did his day trading and wrote poems he published in national journals. Ona, it must be said, made a spare living writing a horoscope column for the local newspaper and doing occasional private readings for individuals of his acquaintance.

Betsy Edger would tell Ona she loved him but could not erase her desire for Shelby, who made her feel pampered and filthy and expected her to do things she had only read about in books or peeked at on the Internet. When she left Shelby to return to Ona Frame's apartment, she would roll her eyes in an agony of guilt and say that she loved Ona for his unimaginative steadiness, that she thought he would be the one to father her children, that with Shelby it was only about sex and the fact that he could help her get her stories published. To both men, she said her behaviour was uncharacteristic, that she had never been with two lovers at once, that she knew she had to decide.

Ona Frame adored her honesty. He felt that no one had ever levelled with him in such an extraordinarily forthright manner. But then her eyes would dip, she would cross and uncross her legs and adjust her bra straps, and he would know that she was thinking of Shelby, would in fact soon abandon him for some *outré* rendezvous. While lovemaking between

Ona and Betsy had dwindled to an occasional hasty encounter in the dark between his fetid sheets, often so mechanical and dispassionate as not to disturb Twinks his cat, sleeping at the foot of the bed, Shelby and Betsy had embarked on a fugue of compulsive exhibitionism and public sex.

Ona Frame himself had recently spotted them fingering each other in the Family Passive Recreation Park at the corner of Route 67 and Middle Line Road while apparently engrossed in doing the Sunday crossword at a picnic table. He had also seen them fondling in a booth at the Dunkin' Donuts and having torrid intercourse only half hidden behind the hydrangeas in Congress Park at dusk.

He had, in fact, developed his own compulsion for following Betsy and Shelby, spending long hours watching Shelby's darkened windows for signs of movement or trailing Shelby's late-model, atrociously undependable BMW as it wound through the streets, watching the two heads in front of him combine and separate then combine once more in a dangerous dance of eros and imminent pedestrian death (or so he thought). Once, he trailed them to the public library where Betsy worked and came upon them masturbating together in the fiction stacks by the letter *M* for, as Ona Frame thought, mischief, menopause, malicious and mad. They paid no heed to Ona or the four or five other readers gawking at them over their books, their eyes fixed on one another, on their pulsing fingers, on the convulsive movements of their thighs, Betsy's left hand wandering strangely over the books at her back, her mouth whispering unintelligible words.

When she arrived at his little bachelor apartment, with the Edvard Munch prints, the dried field-flower bouquets, and his grandmother's yellowing lace doilies, for their regular Thursday night peppermint tea and Scrabble date, Betsy was as prim and collected as ever and made no mention of that afternoon's assignation. But at half past nine, just as Ona had assured himself of victory with an eight-letter triple-word score (*oxymoron*), Betsy emerged from the bathroom clutching at her wristwatch and anxiously announcing that she had to leave. She said Shelby had turned frantically jealous of her relationship with Ona and that she had to get back to him before he did something desperate and self-destructive.

"Self-destructive?" Ona Frame repeated.

"He's capable of anything," she said. "He's been losing in the market. He hasn't written in weeks. He is totally obsessed with me."

Her eyes gave a little dip, which made Ona shudder. Some hint there, he thought, of self-consciousness, of pleasure taken in the drama she was creating. Oh, to have the whole suicidal world of men at your feet, he thought. But it made him love her all the more.

The phone rang. It was Shelby. He asked to speak to Betsy. But Ona held the phone and said, "S., are you desperate and self-destructive?"

And Shelby whispered harshly, "Yes, you idiot. I'm standing on a kitchen stool with a noose around my neck. Put her on."

And Ona waited, thinking, before saying, "No, S., go ahead and hang yourself. I found her first. We can't both love her."

Betsy's expression of frantic agony turned to despair as she ran out, leaving the door open in her wake. There was a tremendous crash at the other end of the line, followed by a lengthy guttural moan, then silence.

Ona Frame hung up the phone, poured himself a thimble of lime vodka from the freezer to calm his shattered nerves, and returned to the horoscope he had been preparing that afternoon. "Scorpio: The path you are on will surely lead to disaster unless you learn flexibility and humility. Avoid ropes. Value old friendships." Shelby was a Scorpio. Ona didn't need to check the star charts to write that one.

An hour later—it was getting late, past ten-thirty—Betsy Edger called from the Emergency Room to say that Shelby was not dead but could not speak above a whisper due to an injury to his throat. She said she needed to stay with Shelby, who was sedated and popping Vicodin for the pain, and also that she was disappointed in Ona for his callous behaviour. She did not think they should see each other again.

When she hung up, a wave of self-pity broke over Ona Frame. It had been the same with the luminous small-time movie actress. When she deigned to bless him with her presence, even if it were only to express her contempt, he was euphoric and cocky. But then she would punish him by going to Shelby, and he would be grief-stricken, terrified at her absence. Her absence made him love her all the more desperately.

It seemed to him that Betsy Edger had gradually taken on an air of luminosity not unlike that of the small-time actress. And she had begun alluding to a drug-filled past, occasionally disappearing from both Ona and Shelby only to explain later, somewhat enigmatically, that she had been at a "meeting," while insisting that she herself was not an addict. Indeed, he had begun to detect a frenzied dis-ease gradually infiltrating Betsy Edger's calm self-possession; or perhaps, he thought, he was only beginning to notice the effort it took her to be calm and self-possessed, while underneath there churned a vast ocean of obsession, self-hatred, impulsiveness, and grandiose fantasies.

At first, he put this down to Shelby's malign influence. Shelby was a lovely man, Ona's best friend since college, when they had both briefly dated the same charmingly accident-prone field hockey player. But around women, Shelby's dark side erupted. He encouraged them to liberate themselves, act outrageously, and transgress convention; the only life was constant change, he said. With Shelby, women turned into libidinal monsters of aberrant desire, nymphs of catastrophe, even on casual first dates.

These women would then drive Shelby crazy because, despite all signs to the contrary, he was a man of habit and routine. But, to Ona Frame's discredit, these chaotic women—he thought of them as Shelby's creations—invariably fascinated him. Easily bored, he found he needed catastrophe in his life. When you hit a bump, he thought, you know you're awake.

In a moment of cruel candour, the small-time actress (her name was Majory Sass) had admitted to Ona Frame that she was addicted to pornographic sex with Shelby, although it disgusted her even when she was "getting off." She said, "He only comes when I tell him what I do with you and I touch him with my fingers." Hearing the words, Ona had descended into a delirium of sadness, self-reproach, and hatred even as he discovered himself in possession of what Shelby liked to call a throbbing bone-daddy and threw himself upon Majory Sass, who took him avidly, with an expression of pity and contempt on her virtuous features.

Ona Frame thought of the days that followed Shelby's suicide attempt as an interregnum, a hiatus, a breathing space. He had experienced many such in the past, during the Majory-Sass-small-time-movie-actress episode, for example, but also in earlier (now that he thought of it) chapters in his long and conflicted relationship with Shelby, who, it must be said, seemed to feed off Ona Frame's pathetic shadow existence, who seemed to need a failed doppelgänger as a sign of his success in life.

During this period, Ona Frame did not see Betsy Edger except, of course, when he went to the library and spied on her or obsessively drove by Shelby's apartment, occasionally catching a glimpse of their furtive shadows against the windows.

On the third day, he received a postcard from Betsy, a reproduction of Edvard Munch's *The Scream* (exactly the same as the print over his bed) and the words: "Ona, Please stop following me. I think we should leave each other alone for a while. Love, Majory."

He marvelled at the cavalier insouciance of her cruelty. She, who had incited, even encouraged his compulsive passion, now pretended to be the virtuously aggrieved victim of his unwelcome attentions. Whereas he knew, he knew, because she had told him, that she "got off" while being watched in the act of love (on five or ten occasions, mostly with strangers). Although now he was not sure if it was Betsy Edger or Majory Sass or someone else entirely who had told him the stories.

It alarmed him to realize that he had misread the signature at the bottom of the message, that it in fact did say "Betsy" and not "Majory." Although from time to time he would snatch a terrified peek, and it would read "Majory" and not "Betsy," so that he could never be sure which was real and which he imagined.

And it was difficult for him to give up his spying because he was addicted to the sudden submissive rush, the flood of near-orgasmic bliss, that accompanied each decision to humiliate himself, to break with the conventions of manhood, self-respect, and dignity. Every moment of secretive observation was an agony of not wanting to be caught and wanting to be caught.

But Ona Frame, with a heroic effort, managed to reduce his library visits to five or six a day, and only spent eight hours and thirty-four minutes outside Shelby's apartment over the next two nights—mostly because he fell asleep the second night. (He dreamed of watching Betsy Edger deliver a baby; in the dream, the baby had Shelby's face and the doctor was also Shelby, and he, Ona Frame, when he looked in a mirror, was Shelby.)

He spent his spare time trying to write a poem that he thought would impress Betsy, who was always going on about what a wonderful poet Shelby was, how it was his mind that turned her on sexually, while Ona Frame, who could only tell the future, could not write a poem to save his life.

He knew that it was Shelby's habit to be especially self-absorbed and productive after a suicide attempt. Yes, there had been earlier failed self-murders. Shelby was a habitual attention-seeker, a perverse dramatist of macabre exits at which he was incompetent. But these dismal attempts somehow freed his heart to write exquisite poems of which, prior to killing himself, in the ordinary course of his life, he was incapable.

Ona Frame knew, too, there would be no *outré* sexual shenanigans *chez* Shelby, that Betsy Edger would grow bored in her role as the virtuous nurse of an intensely concentrated poet who paid attention to words and not to her, that by telling Ona to stop coming around she had put an end to her only source of distraction, that the whole exercise would expose the emptiness at the centre of her life, which their love triangle had hidden from her.

He imagined that she might try to work on her own writing, which he knew had not produced much except for, yes, conventionally enough, a terse fragment dealing with her abortion years before and a pornographic scene involving two men in a storage room above a Subway in lower Manhattan. Shelby said Betsy Edger's chief fault as a writer was an inability to lie, just as her chief fault as a person was an inability to tell the truth. Which Ona Frame took to be a harshly unjust summation of their mutual love's shortcomings, though, as usual, he admired Shelby's linguistic panache.

But at the time, during the interregnum, when, in fact,

Betsy was staying with Shelby exclusively, Ona Frame continued to write bad poems, struggled with his stalking addiction, foretold the future, and alternately hated Betsy Edger and thrilled to fantasies of torrid sexual congress. Though, in truth, after titillating him with stories of wild exhibitionism, swinger sex, mischievous infidelities, and rare fetishes, she had confessed to preferring the missionary position while also claiming she had never had an orgasm that way. She only had orgasms when she was by herself.

With such contradictory signals emanating from the one he loved, Ona Frame had felt sexually whipsawed. All desire had left him except the desire to conform his desire to Betsy Edger's desires, which were, in the end, incomprehensible. He had felt himself being sucked into an infinite regress of assertion and contradiction that left him trembling and powerless, a state which he adored. With Betsy Edger gone and her sternly written admonition to stay away tacked to the otherwise empty corkboard above his kitchen table, he was in an ecstasy, sure only of his passion and, yes, that Betsy Edger would return. He was, as he thought, only awaiting new instructions.

It was a Wednesday evening, late, about ten o'clock, and Ona Frame was tucked up in bed with Twinks the cat wrapped around his head like a hat, when he heard a tentative tap at the door. He had some trouble getting up, Twinks refusing to relinquish his perch and scratching Ona Frame's forehead. A trail of blood beads erupted down the bridge of his nose. He had an erection tangled in his L.L. Bean flannel nightshirt. (He had, of course, been dreaming of Majory Sass or Betsy Edger or perhaps the accident-prone field hockey player—whose name, by the way, was Emma Christmas.)

When she saw his nightshirt-tent, Betsy Edger gave him a triumphant half smile, self-satisfied and libidinous. She said she had missed him but that they could only be friends. Sex was out of the question, she said, her head dipping slightly as she glanced at his diminishing erection. She seemed beautiful in that prim librarian sort of way, with her hair neatly bobbed, no makeup, and a skirt that came to her knees.

"But we can be kind to one another," she added.

Naturally, Ona Frame thought. Naturally, sex will be out of the question. As long as I desire her, she no longer needs to give in to my desires.

Long ago, he had wondered if she was happy, playing this endless push-me-pull-you game of desire and denial, playing the two men off against each other, never giving either precisely what he wanted. He wondered if she was happy since, in fact, she never seemed to get what she wanted either, lived only for the sake of inciting and denying desire in others, for the anhedonic bliss of the chase—a woman's fate.

"Friends," he said. "Yes, of course. Only friends."

She glanced at him with a malicious gleam in her eye (or so it seemed to Ona Frame). "I haven't been totally candid with you, Ona," she said.

"No?" he said weakly.

"When we were still together, I had an affair—that night I spent in New York when I went to my brother's concert."

"Oh," said Ona Frame, thinking, What part of being friends and kind did I not understand?

He felt the bellows of passion fanning his rage, his love, his self-disgust. His erection fought to rise against the L.L. Bean nightshirt. He pawed meekly at Betsy Edger's arm. She twisted away, though she seemed not to be paying attention in any case. She was leafing through his mail on the bookshelf.

"And there were a couple of others. I forget when," she said. "Have you been seeing anyone? Anything to confess on your side?"

Ona Frame shook his head.

"What about the little high school slut who stacks books sometimes? You had your dirty little eyes on her."

"No, no," said Ona Frame, suddenly embarrassed, who, in truth, had been watching the high school girl, who seemed anything but a slut, while he was simultaneously spying on Betsy Edger. He marvelled at how Betsy Edger divined his innermost thoughts and how different she seemed now from the untalented, mousy, demure, naive, ingenuous, quiet girl he had fallen for at the outset. Even her breasts seemed larger.

He had briefly entertained fantasies that the high-school-girl-cum-book-stacker might save him from Betsy Edger and Shelby and Majory Sass (who was rarely out of his mind), not to mention Emma Christmas (also rarely out of his mind—his mind dense with the detritus of old loves, fragmentary memories of pussy, orgasm, armpit smell, sharp retort, cunning absences, glances, gusts of cruel laughter, sobs). And in truth, he had once invited her for a coffee at Virgil's Roast House, where they played backgammon for an hour.

After, he had shyly taken her hand as they walked through the night toward her apartment on Beekman. She was the kind of girl he was always looking for: restrained, demure, monosyllabic, undemanding, attentive.

At her door, he remembered now, the girl had kissed him, the tiny stiff hairs on her upper lip scraping his skin as they touched tongue tips. She had invited him in and offered him Sleepytime tea but opened a bottle of wine instead and drank from the bottle and went to her bedroom to change and came back wearing nothing and kissed him hungrily and turned her back to him so that he took her from behind and came touching herself, moaning, "I love you," which filled Ona Frame with dread and prognostication (he could tell, he could always tell, how things would turn out).

In the drowsy aftermath of sex, she said she had left high school two years before and was trying to be a writer, which was why she liked working in the library. She met men on Match.com and slept with them on the first date. This was the first time the library had worked for her.

Women, too. When she was drunk, she would lose her inhibitions (What inhibitions? Ona Frame wondered) and start kissing whoever was sitting next to her. Once, she had let a man finger her to an orgasm in a booth at Orphan Annie's. She was sure other bar patrons had noticed. She said, "You like hearing this, don't you? My last lover said I give good story." She said it with bravado, with a mischievous gleam in her eyes.

Ona Frame had told no one about the book-stacker, especially not Shelby (for obvious reasons) or Betsy Edger (for even more obvious reasons), and he was sure no one had seen him. Although, if truth be told, he invariably felt as though someone were following him. He was forever glancing over his shoulder, half expecting to find Shelby's BMW hovering at a discreet distance, partly shrouded in exhaust fumes.

During the Majory Sass episode, the so-called "Regrettable Incident," there had been occasions when Ona Frame felt certain Shelby was following him while he was in the act of following Shelby. Once, Ona Frame had thought, We are never going to stop following each other round and round this block. We have entered some mythic space of perpetual mutual stalking.

Betsy Edger's brow suddenly clouded as if she had been reading his thoughts. A flash of anger erupted in her tannin-coloured eyes. "You disgust me," she said, and swept out of the apartment.

Ona Frame clutched himself through the cloth of his L.L. Bean nightshirt and fell to his knees. He began to howl with loneliness and pain, with the horror of abandonment, with amazement at how low he had sunk. Twinks, terrified, crept into a corner under the bed.

But Ona Frame had never been happier, had never felt so alive. He thought, Now I know what it's like to be a fictitious character in a story, that sense of chockablock crisis and fate, of another hand stoking the drama to see how I might perform. At length, he stretched out on the floor, sobbing with gratitude; all Betsy Edger's visit meant was that she still needed him. She needed someone to whom to be cruel, and she had picked Ona. For this he was grateful.

He took three or four vodkas, trying to calm down and

sleep, but telephoned the high school book-stacker instead.

She said, "I met a friend of yours the other day. At least, he said he was a friend of yours, even though he was trying to get into my pants."

Ona Frame put his hand to his heart and felt the shattered rhythms of distress. Her words filled him with sudden dread for the future, for the ridiculous indignity and injustice of aging and death, for the loss of love, which was infinitely more certain than love itself, for the communality of desire, which is never singular but feeds off the desires of others, for the eternal oscillating engine of intimacy that never achieves rest.

Anticipating her answer, he whispered, "Did you— "

And she said, "Listen, baby, love is like the telephone—more than one can use the line."

Her name was Amanda Hawk.

That night, Ona Frame had a nightmare. It began with a tap at the door and then Majory Sass accusing him of having an affair with Betsy Edger. He felt like a little boy caught in the act of masturbating by his stern librarian mother with her tweed skirts and her creamy blouses (with the Dutch collars) buttoned to her throat—oh, how he had adored her. When he woke up, he was not sure he was awake or if the nightmare were merely an extension of the day. His mother had been a high school history teacher, he recalled, not a librarian. She had a face like a stone. It reminded him of someone else's face, but the name escaped him.

Then he wanted to show Shelby a poem he had written. He took the elevator to Shelby's floor but realized, as he rang the doorbell, that he'd forgotten the slip of paper with the poem. And in any case, it wasn't Shelby's building. Trying to leave, he found himself in a maze. He couldn't get out and he couldn't remember the poem. (Sometime during this sequence of events, Ona Frame intuited that he was not awake at all. He wondered if he was ever awake, if such a state existed, or if in fact he was dead, a suicide, dreaming of doubles and things he had forgotten, or if this was the state of mind of a character whose author has forgotten about him.)

Sipping his third morning vodka (he noticed the muzzy dawn light scattering the dirty crepuscules of night in the backyard), he realized how bizarre his life had become. He realized that nothing added up, nothing that happened to him became a story, because time didn't exist, a fact Shelby had pointed out in an e-mail only the week before, when they were still on speaking terms though angry with one another.

"You predict the future in your horoscopes," Shelby had written, "but if you can predict the future, then there is no future, and if there is no future, then there is no time, and if there is no time, then nothing changes and life ceases to exist, only eddies and loops, endlessly trying to start but covering the same ground again and again. Without time, there is only repetition. You are hysterically frightened of time, aging and death, Ona Frame, but the poet knows you can't live without them. You can't abide a paradox. This is why Betsy Edger loves me more than she loves you."

The words had confused Ona Frame because he was only

twenty-six years old and because Shelby also dabbled in horoscopes. Indeed, Shelby had often filled in for Ona Frame when Ona ran out of inspiration. Shelby had once said there was little difference between writing horoscopes and writing poetry and that they were both like talking to a woman you love, the woman of your dreams.

Shelby also had a terrible habit of repeating himself, telling the same stories again and again. Sometimes they were stories Ona Frame had told Shelby a moment before.

That afternoon, Ona Frame ran into Shelby and Betsy Edger at the Price Chopper, temple of food. It was hardly an accident because he had been following them since dawn, when he woke up and discovered Shelby's ineffable BMW wheezing exhaust fumes outside Amanda Hawk's apartment house.

Ona Frame was behind in his horoscopes. His editor had threatened to fire him. His credit cards were maxed out. He drank vodka in the morning to calm his shattered nerves. Then he drank more in the afternoon and evening. He had spent the night having revenge sex with Marion Esterhazy, a newbie playwright and dysfunctional book-stacker at the library, who said revenge sex is the best next to breakup sex. (Although Ona Frame was not sure if he was avenging himself against Shelby or Betsy Edger or Majory Sass or someone else entirely.)

As they wrestled on Marion Esterhazy's stale, well-used sheets, he had written an entire lyric poem in his head.

But when he woke up, he was sitting in his car outside Amanda Hawk's apartment with no idea how or why he was there except that he must have been spying on someone.

Shelby had once said that in life actions are often motivated by nothing more than boredom and banality, which, only in retrospect, take on the character of personality or fate or divine guidance.

Shelby also said the kind of woman you choose is an expression of your attitude to life.

Ona Frame thought, But Shelby only chooses women I want to be with. Or is it that I am only attracted to women Shelby would be attracted to? As always for Ona Frame, thought itself was a vertiginous experience.

The sight of the BMW filled him with happiness and despair. Briefly, he had thought he might have Amanda Hawk all to himself, whereas with Betsy Edger (not to mention Majory Sass) he had quickly recognized a tendency to insecure attachment. But a tendency to insecure attachment seemed to be contagious, or it was the modern thing, or it was the subterranean essence of love.

Oh, he thought, we are always looking for our one true love, but invariably she suffers from a tendency to insecure attachment, or has slept with thirty-three other strangers through Match.com, or wants to share herself with your best friend. Perfection eludes us. We are doomed to disappointment and negotiation. The other is always, *always*, someone else.

Ona Frame had watched in horror tinged with satisfaction as the newly luminous Amanda Hawk descended her plank stoop and let herself into the BMW. He had not tried to conceal his presence, driving just behind the BMW, once nudging its rear fender at a stoplight. (He had a theory that if you stalked openly, it wasn't stalking any more, only an intimate friendship.)

He had trailed the couple to the Family Passive Recreation Park (an old trysting ground, which Ona Frame had discovered with Emma Christmas one Christmas), then Virgil's Roast House, the library, and Shelby's apartment. Sometimes Ona Frame found himself driving ahead of the BMW, or so it seemed. Again, it occurred to him that the roles had reversed and Shelby was following him. At the library, Amanda Hawk jumped out of the car without waiting for it to come to a full stop, glared at Shelby, spat words Ona Frame could not hear, then slammed the door getting back in. At the Family Passive Recreation Park, Shelby attempted to have finger sex while pretending to do the Sunday crossword, but this only erupted in an argument.

In the Price Chopper, Ona spied from behind a pyramid display of Bush's Baked Beans as Betsy Edger marched Shelby through the organic foods. There was something simian about Shelby's affect, in the way he crouched beside her, swinging his arms below his knees. He wore a winter scarf, though it was midsummer, no doubt to conceal the livid blue weal that betrayed his recent suicide attempt. His pupils were dilated, from the Vicodin, Ona Frame thought (he had long known of Shelby's flirtations with addiction, how he loved gum surgery, for example, for the painkillers after).

Shelby seemed afraid of Betsy Edger, often winced when she turned to address him. When he spoke, she had to lean down to hear his hoarse whispers and often seemed impatient at having to do so.

Once, when Shelby's wandering glance seemed to focus in Ona Frame's direction, Ona Frame offered a tentative wave and a nod of his head and then pushed his cart into a parallel aisle. (He had absent-mindedly loaded the cart with plastic cartons of sliced pineapple, overripe avocados, and super-economy-size maxi-pads.)

Shelby cornered him breathlessly by the breath mints. He looked worse, more desperate, up close, also sinister, if not malevolent. His florid face seemed ready to explode into flame. (There had always been a struggle with high blood pressure, which Ona Frame assumed would one day be the end of Shelby, given his incompetence at killing himself.)

In a barely audible whisper, so soft that Ona Frame had to lean into his friend's face to hear the words, Shelby said, "She's insatiable. Ona, get out while you can. Save yourself. She's been talking about leaving me for you. I can't bear the contempt in her voice."

And Ona Frame said, "Been writing, have you? You always look like this when you're doing your best work." He pitched his voice to sound affable but barely concealed a sneer.

Shelby caught himself in full paranoid flight and took a breath. He said, "Why, no. You know I can't write when things are like this. She'll destroy me before I write anything worthwhile again. You're the one who always comes up with something brilliant when the situation has turned to cinders and ashes. Remember what happened after Majory Sass?"

Ona Frame was taken aback at this outright denial of what he knew to be true. It was Shelby who was hooked on love, who wrote on love, who needed the brutal excitement of the mutual psychic invasion that is love in order to create. True, Ona Frame's Majory Sass poem had been published, not his first either. But he had never been in Shelby's class, never considered himself a real writer. He foretold the future—not very well. There were often complaints from irate readers who foolishly took his advice.

Shelby said, "She says we look alike. Even our you-know-whats are the same, she says. She says that with the lights out, she can't tell who she's with. It enrages me. It's as if I don't exist. You know she only comes when she's by herself."

The two men dragged cases of bottled water off the shelf and, using the maxi-pads as cushions, made themselves comfortable in the aisle. Shelby asked Ona Frame for a cigarette, which he fitted into a six-inch amber holder and lit with a monogrammed lighter (OF for Ona Frame—Shelby had stolen the lighter but refused to acknowledge it). He lit one for Ona Frame as well, although Ona Frame rarely smoked except under stress, which, when he thought about it, was most of the time. Ona Frame expected someone to object, but many shoppers seemed delighted to see a pair of desperate outlaws in their midst. Several asked for cigarettes as well. A blue haze, a fog of smoke, drifted into the steel rafters.

Someone offered them a beer, and someone else broke out the Planters Deluxe Mixed Nuts. A conversation erupted that had nothing to do with Betsy Edger or love or shopping but seemed, insofar as Ona Frame paid attention, to be about Schopenhauer's aesthetics, or perhaps it was Schoenberg's atonal music. A joint began to make the rounds as more and more shoppers joined in. Gusts of laughter swept the aisle.

A tiny black-haired woman, with spectacles on a garnet chain, peered over her lenses and said, "You are Frame, the poet. I recognize you."

A pair of young lovers stood to one side watching, smiling to themselves. The girl was pregnant. She seemed radiantly happy and took the boy's hand, whispering something in his ear, and he blushed and kissed her hard suddenly.

Ona Frame and Shelby could see Majory Sass flirting with a checkout boy, a teenager, at the foot of the aisle. At a distance, her face animated, a good-natured smile playing across her broad, appealing features, a hand now and then dragging through her bobbed hair, she seemed beautiful, guileless and innocent, not the infernal succubus they had come to know so well.

Ona Frame whispered hoarsely, imitating Shelby, "She's very good with strangers. She calls it her 'ongoing conversation with the world.' It's charming. Have you got any of that Vicodin left?"

"OxyContin is better," said Shelby. "You know, my back doesn't hurt any more, either."

"Mine is killing me," said Ona Frame, "especially after last night."

"Actually, nothing hurts any more," said Shelby, an uncertainly optimistic smile beginning to play across his features.

Time passed. Although neither man believed in time. So it passed very quickly.

They talked of love and poetry in the old way, watching Majory Sass, who seemed to be exchanging e-mail addresses or phone numbers with the checkout boy.

Someone had replaced the Price Chopper muzak with a Stevie Ray Vaughan selection. Shelby loosened his scarf. He said something about the magical charm of atmospheres, how things might change for no reason except that you suddenly felt better, because of Stevie Ray Vaughan and a little 420 action in Price Chopper and customers turning into people, against all odds, and holding conversations. Although you could never write a story like that.

"You must introduce me to your new girl," Shelby said, throwing the tail of his scarf over his shoulder with panache. "I'm sure she's wonderful."

"I don't know," said Ona Frame. "She reminds me of someone. It might not work out." He fingered the broken, raised scar at his throat, wondered why he was suddenly whispering.

Betsy Edger (or was it someone else entirely?) was helping the checkout boy with the bagging and gently humouring a dour, waspish-looking, elderly woman with arms like sticks and eyes like cudgels.

"All the best stories end with a wedding," said Shelby. "Think of Shakespeare."

Ona Frame thought, *Hamlet*, *King Lear*, *Macbeth*? He didn't like it when Shelby turned manic and expansive, the usual prelude to Shelby stealing Ona's girl. But there was also something appealing in the new mood.

Suddenly, Shelby rose to his feet and began organizing stoned Price Chopper customers. An altar improvised with crates of Bush's Baked Beans cans appeared in the aisle. He threw his scarf over it like a cloth and motioned the young pregnant couple (still kissing) to come forward. A towering fat man, the shape of a gourd, in khaki cargo pants, checked shirt and Tilley hat, with a beaming face, stood up for the bride. Betsy Edger drifted in at the back of the congregation, arm in arm with the teenage checkout boy. She looked about his age, which made Ona Frame wonder if he ever saw anything the way it really was. She pushed the checkout boy forward, and he stood by the groom, awkward and shy, but pleased with his sudden ascension. He wore a blue Price Chopper polo shirt and a name tag that read, *Brad, Front-End.*

He could have been the groom's brother, they looked that much alike.

Shelby began to intone the order of service, what he could remember of it. Sometimes Ona Frame would have to whisper a correction or fill in a gap.

"Dearly beloved," he began, "we are gathered together today in the sight of God—"

And between the two of them, they managed to get through the entire ceremony with only a slip here and there, Shelby's voice growing deeper and stronger, soaring, as he went. And Ona Frame found himself caught up in the words, which he had heard before, the old words, that seemed to point at some human meaning he could no longer access. "...holy Matrimony; which is an honourable estate, instituted by God in the time of man's innocency..." He felt wistful about that (and wondered when the time of man's innocency was), wistful about Betsy Edger, who, when he glanced at her, was positively luminous. "...for the mutual society, help, and comfort that the one ought to have for the other..." The crowd of shoppers, though they knew they were only pretending, grew into their roles as bridesmaids, ushers, mothers, fathers, cousins, uncles, best friends of bride or groom, old classmates. "Wilt thou love her, comfort her, honour and keep her, in sickness and in health; and, forsaking all other, keep thee only unto her, so long as you both shall live?" Ona Frame noticed that the marriage service mentioned nothing about a tendency to insecure attachment and remembered countless times he had misremembered that phrase as "as long as you both shall love." Or perhaps, he thought, that was the modern translation, meant to accommodate all those tendencies to insecure attachment. The young couple exchanged rings from a costume in the seasonal aisle, and when Shelby said he could, the blushing groom kissed the blushing bride, a chaste and adoring kiss, almost a first kiss (leaving out the pregnancy that made straight-on hugging difficult). Grown men wept and said they had never attended a more moving ceremony. Betsy Edger ran up and kissed the checkout boy, as if kissing were suddenly contagious. Onlookers enthusiastically shook Ona Frame's hand and congratulated him. He didn't know why. He had tears in his eyes. He didn't know why he had tears in his eyes. Someone said there would be a reception by the cold beer. The black-haired, garnet-chained poetry reader asked him if he would be giving the speech. "Yes, yes," he said. "Of course." Although normally he was terrified of public speaking, which was Shelby's forte. Anything seemed possible suddenly. He had spotted a young woman in the crowd, dark hair bobbed, plain determined face, nothing luminous but something strong inwardly, a quiet, undemanding girl for whom the words "comfort" and "honour" and "innocency" might really mean something. He made his way through the throng, a small poem forming on his lips, or a horoscope. Out of the corner of his eye, he spotted Shelby surging in the same direction. But then Shelby stopped, something stopped him. He smiled at Ona Frame, and turned away.

Pointless, Incessant Barking in the Night

I went to the hospital to visit my neighbour Geills after her suicide attempt. She explained that she had used a generic brand of garbage bag, which tore inconveniently along a seam, and that she had been in love with me since we met in the alley behind our houses the night the dog barked.

I remembered that night for its knot of misunderstandings and embarrassments. Susan, my wife, had been asleep in the bedroom. I was working late on my dissertation in the breakfast nook, still wearing my teaching uniform, tie and a cardigan with leather patches on the elbows, my glasses smeared with powdered sugar from the doughnuts I habitually ate when I was working. She misinterpreted the sugar traces as evidence of a drug habit, which intrigued her. She also thought my late-night tie wearing was symptomatic of a deep fetish attachment, perhaps an interesting S&M thing, she said later.

For my part, when I realized it was her dog we were searching for, I began to berate her for disturbing her neighbours in the middle of the night. She began to weep, twisting her chubby little hands in the lap of her T-shirt nightie, dragging it off her shoulder and revealing the butterfly tattoo, which alarmed me with its suggestiveness. In the silence that followed, we both heard the dog again, now baying woefully a block or two away. I said good night, wishing to cut short this evening of cross-purposes, and left her scurrying through the weathered plank gate that led into her backyard.

I was brushing my teeth when she came knocking tentatively at my back door. She had locked herself out of the little basement apartment she rented from the Wallingfords, two doors down. She didn't want to wake them. I was the only person she knew in the neighbourhood who was awake. She couldn't go walking around dressed as she was. It was too chilly to wait outside till sun-up. She said her name was Geills. She inadvertently showed me her tattoo again. She balanced first on one foot and then on the other (bare feet) in my mud room. We could hear the dog, almost at the foot of the yard, howling, wolflike. She had blue hair—I didn't know it was blonde underneath till later—and a gleaming ball on her tongue that flashed as she rolled her eyes anxiously.

I could not bear the anxiety she seemed to feel. I ushered her into my kitchen and brought her a blanket and a pair of slippers and made English Breakfast tea in a pot with two cups though I wasn't intending to drink any myself. I poured her a small schnapps, but she refused it. She seemed almost afraid, shivering violently across the little nook table from me. There were papers strewn all around. Distracted, I read a half-finished sentence on a torn scrap: "The most beautiful and melancholy line in all literature, the summa of love..."

Clumsily wrapping herself in the blanket, she swept the pages onto the floor, then I caught a glimpse of her pale nipples when she knelt to pick them up. There was some tension in the air, something indefinable, set off earlier by that pointless, incessant barking in the night. I said not to worry about the papers. I had jumped up so violently that my chair fell to the floor with a crash loud enough, I was certain, to wake Susan, my wife. Geills stepped into my arms urgently but also as if it were the natural thing to do. I was relieved to feel her shivering subside. But then I noticed that I was shivering.

She said, "You know we look alike."

I couldn't think what she meant.

She said, "You can do whatever you want." She peered up at me with timid eyes that seemed all sclera.

It would have been heartless to refuse, though, in the event, I cannot think why I abandoned my habitual circumspection in that moment. Something to do with the dark of night and that incessant barking, which seemed to mock the reason and orderliness of day. Geills climbed onto the breakfast nook bench on her hands and knees and I took her from behind like a dog, neither of us able to see the other's face, both lost in some private erotic dementia, submitting not to one another but the moment, the act itself, submitting to submission, willing the universal catastrophe.

I had the sensation of being in a dream, driving a car fast along some impossible hairpin zigzag of a road, completely out of control but also somehow certain that if I just kept going very fast, nothing bad would happen to me. I came with a shout, upsetting the teapot onto the floor, smashing it (still Susan, my wife, didn't wake).

Geills kissed me once and whispered, "Please, don't regret this."

And then I remember practically nothing until about sunrise when Susan, my wife, came downstairs and found the broken teapot and Geills curled up asleep on the floor with the blanket and me equally asleep with my head on my arms at the breakfast nook table. I woke to the reek of schnapps and the snap of Susan's cigarette lighter (she had stopped smoking but liked to snap the lighter in stressful situations) and the semi-conscious realization that I was not who I thought I was. Susan was about to realize this as well, and the entire constellation of essences and relations that had constituted our marriage, which had hitherto seemed immutable, was about to go smash. But I was determined not to be humiliated by the situation (difficult, given that my pants were still around my ankles).

I said, gesturing with my hand, "This is exactly what it looks like."

"How long has it been going on?" she asked.

I peered at my watch. "About three hours," I said.

"I mean how long has *this* been going on?" she repeated, nodding at Geills, who was beginning to stir.

"Three hours," I said. "I'm certain because I checked my watch when the dog was barking."

I thought, Is this what love is like? So desperate, so catastrophic? Susan looked at me as if surprised by my thoughts.

Geills said, "Oh shit." Her tone gently ironic, as if this were the usual thing, the usual morning-after mess.

She wrapped the blanket around her breasts, which were trying to make another escape from her nightie. She glared at Susan, which I took to be a defensive gesture, an act of defiance. But then Susan faltered. Her face went suddenly vague, a kind of indeterminate softening engendered by confusion and doubt. Once, she had confided to me that when her mother read her bedtime stories, she had left all the love scenes out. We had been married four or five years, and the marriage had fallen into a dispassionate routine, two people running on separate, parallel tracks for the last—what?—four or five years. So that nothing should have surprised her, except, I suppose, finding a blue-haired, tattooed, naked teenager in her kitchen at six a.m. on a weekday (not to mention her husband with his pants around his ankles).

She snapped her lighter once or twice more and then shivered so hard that she needed to wrap her arms around her shoulders to control it. (The shivering seemed to pass from one to the other, I thought, like the symptom of an infectious disease, like a possession, like the touch of angel wings.) Susan shrugged vaguely, then swept abruptly out of the kitchen and retreated upstairs toward the bedroom.

"Shit," said Geills. "Do you love her?" she asked.

I thought for a moment, pulling my pants up, a humble, universal moment. For that moment, I was Everyman, every man who had ever been tested by God and a blue-haired woman in his kitchen.

"Yes," I said, "I must. I must have. I married her. Isn't that why you get married?"

Geills furrowed her brow and peered down her nose at me as though she feared for my sanity. I could see what she was thinking.

She tried to kill herself later in the week, was found unconscious in her bed by a friend known only by the monosyllabic nickname Frag, who sometimes slept there on what she later assured me was a non-sexual basis except for a blow job now and then when he was needy. That afternoon I cancelled my Proust seminar (another story of difficult love) and took the hospital elevator up to the third floor, where the doctors had placed her in an observation ward with several other incompetent suicides, three of whom were playing a noisy game of Monopoly when I walked in.

She said, "How did you find me? This place is kept secret. The elevator skips this floor. It has no number."

I said, "That's ridiculous. I came up the elevator."

She said, "If you're going to be my lover, you have to stop being so literal."

I had not seen her since the fateful night, though every day I had walked through the alley and knocked on her door in vain. Not only that, but Susan had asked me to leave, and Geills could not have missed the rented van parked on the tree lawn all Thursday afternoon as I hefted crates of books, a Morris chair, a reading lamp with a swing arm and counterweight, a laptop computer, and my file boxes of acid-free manila folders out of the house.

"Look," she said, "this gown thingy they gave me has no back."

I said, "Stop that."

She said, "It's depressing in here. They put me in with all these geeks who are trying to kill themselves."

I admit I was a little breathless. These were more words than we had yet exchanged, not that many of them made sense, and she was lying on the hospital bed on her belly with the back of her gown spread wide and her buttocks slightly elevated.

I said, "Do you have anyone? Is there anybody who can help?"

Someone at the Monopoly board used the word "rebarbative" in a sentence, which made me want to investigate, made me feel ever so slightly schizophrenic. The whole place had a menacing and miasmatic air, something like a summer camp for very depressed people, with special workshops for hysterical mourning, melancholy silences, and impotence, much like the college where I taught, much like the house I lived in, like the house I had grown up in, like my life—a place where you could play board games and talk about love till you got so downhearted you had to jump out a window.

"I love you madly," she said.

"Really, you don't know me," I said.

"I know everything I need to know," she said. "But you should have told me you were married before you led me on like that." I gave her a look. "Just kidding," she said.

The cheeks of her buttocks squeezed together impishly. I caught myself drifting into reprehensible fancies. I extended a forefinger and ran it up and down between her cheeks. She craned her neck to gaze at me, eyes glossy with tears, wonder, and sudden terror. Her breath came in quick, fluttering whispers, the bellows of arousal.

But she said, "Don't start something you're not going to finish."

I thought, She is beautiful in a bobbed, blue-haired, tattooed, chunky teenager-ish sort of way. I thought, Am I insane?

"I know what you're thinking," she said.

I explained about moving out, about how I was sleeping in a rental storage unit by the malls and showering at the college gym. I was surprised to see how many unattached men lived in rental storage units. I owned a little spirit stove I used for cooking in my shared office at the college. She said I could move in with her.

"What about Frag?" I asked.

"He's cool," she said.

I didn't know what she meant. Did that mean Frag would move out, or would he merely acquiesce to sharing Geills with me? So far I had only heard about Frag, but I remembered seeing a dirty, bearded man in a fatigue jacket loitering in the neighbourhood. I associated him with the barking dog, car alarms going off in the night, terrified old ladies behind locked doors.

Someone behind me said the word "lobotomy." And I thought of the dog, how its pointless, incessant barking had first drawn us into the night and then driven us to adultery in the breakfast nook. I thought of her tattoo.

"Show me the butterfly," I said.

I thought how this was the most exciting thing that had happened to me so far, and I thought that actually not much had ever happened to me. I thought of Susan, my wife, and the mysteries of love and marriage, how once I had adored her, albeit in a tepid way, how habit is the death of the heart. Though now, as I stood there with my finger in Geills's ass, I remembered how Susan had been the instigator, how in fact she had regarded me, in a small way, as a trophy husband. She liked it that I had enough degrees to paper a wall and that her friend Diane would always be saying, "I can't talk in front of your husband because he'll think I am stupid." (Though subsequently I learned that Diane thought I was a bore.) But then the evening after she discovered me with Geills (with my pants around my ankles) in the kitchen, Susan said that I had betrayed her and that she had lost the element of trust essential to our relationship. She went on, but the general drift was such that I thought, She doesn't know what to say. She is speaking from a script and cannot access what is true and real in her heart. I felt sorry for her, though when she began hectoring me on property division, spousal maintenance, and child support—"What children?" "I might have some later," she said—I began to feel less sorry. At some point, I said, "I'll move." Susan seemed at a loss. She seemed to want the conversation to continue, dreary and dispiriting as it was.

*

Frag had promised to drive Geills home from the hospital but did not show up, and she called me on my cell in the middle of my Proust seminar makeup class. Akoschka Weatherby was droning on about Proust and queer theory. She had a hunch, only a hunch, mind you, because she had not read the book or the assigned critical texts or even browsed the Internet for information, a hunch based primarily on five lines of back-flap copy, that Proust was gay and possibly this influenced his writing. Akoschka Weatherby assumed her symmetrical features, healthy bosom, and finely plucked eyebrows would make up for any defect of thought. And she was right in a Proustian sort of way. I had my face in my hands with the tips of my little fingers holding up my eyelids on account of serial nights of insomnia brought on by the barking dog (incessant and pointless), marital discord, career anxiety, questions about the future, and my new friends at the rental storage unit dropping in at all hours to borrow cups of cooking wine.

Out of a sense of duty, I had gone to see Susan. She was very calm though thinner, tighter, obsessively fondling her cigarette lighter; thinner, tighter, as in impossibly so, as in growing denser, as in the universe before the Big Bang. She said it was not so much that I had been conducting an affair behind her back—men being men and all, you expect that kind of thing—but she realized I was squandering energy better spent on my dissertation, my job prospects were dwindling, and I was turning into a disappointment. I said

I was thinking of chucking the dissertation anyway. So far the only person impressed with my academic credentials had been her friend Diane, who didn't like me. Also, Professor Detweiler, chair of the department, had taken my office key away after the fire.

I said, "Have you heard the dog barking, that pointless, incessant barking in the night?"

Susan looked at me as if I were a loon.

After Geills's phone call from the hospital, I told my class I was leaving, not likely to return, and that it was no loss because there wasn't a single one of them with an ounce of talent, insight, or originality, not one capable of rudimentary thought, and only one or two with the ability to put more than three words together to form simple sentences in any language. I said they should all go out and get jobs as office cleaners.

Someone in the back row said, "Right on!" demonstrating that he had not heard a word I said.

As I packed my monogrammed Lands' End briefcase (a gift from Susan, my wife), Ramon Petunless, a colonial studies doctoral candidate of mixed Ethiopian and Puerto Rican heritage, asked if he could have my address in case he needed a recommendation one day. I gave him a business card from the rental storage place, of which I had taken a small stack for keeping notes, and said I would be there for the foreseeable future.

I took a cab to the hospital, where Geills was more than happy to see me, although they would not let her leave until I pretended to be a relative, which was difficult given the enthusiastic and lewd manner in which she embraced me and continued with her arms around me and her crotch pressed into my thigh.

Nurse: "Are you a relative, sir?"

Me: "Ur, yes."

Nurse: "What is your relation to this child, sir?"

Me: "Put down 'sibling.'"

Nurse: Silence pregnant with disapproval.

Me: "Put down 'uncle' then."

Nurse: "All right, sir, but you know it is a federal offence to knowingly and fraudulently give incorrect information to a health official."

Me: "A very distant uncle, an uncle with several removals. I am the brother of her mother's third cousin-in-law by marriage."

Nurse: "Thank you, sir. And what name shall I put?"

Me: "Ramon Petunless."

At this point Geills had her hand down the back of my pants and was heading south.

Me: "Can we leave now?"

Nurse: "You understand that you are responsible for all medical expenses?"

Me: "Sure. How much would that be?"

Geills was dragging me by a belt loop toward the exit, looking more cheerful than she had a right to be.

Nurse: "$22,681.23."

Me: "Gosh. Can you bill me?" I gave her one of my rental storage cards. "I am the owner."

Nurse: "You can't leave like this. She needs to be in a wheelchair till she gets out of the hospital."

Me: "But she can walk. She tried to kill herself with a plastic bag. It didn't damage her legs. Her legs are in perfect working order. It's her mind that's damaged."

Nurse: Silence pregnant with disapproval.

We made love in the back seat of the cab, much to the delight of the driver, a Somali expatriate with an unpronounceable name, a smooth, handsome face, and a tendency to laugh and say, "Oh, boy," when he looked in the rear-view mirror. It was sudden and surprising.

One minute we were discussing Proust and what the French call Monopoly and the next she was saying, "Listen to this," and sticking one of her iPod earplugs in my ear.

"What's this?" I said.

"An iPod," she said. "It's for playing music."

I gave her a look.

"Just kidding," she said. "It's Modest Mouse. You heard them before?"

I had to admit I hadn't. She had the other earplug in her ear and she took my hand and interlaced our fingers and squeezed gently and smiled with a sort of contentment, and I kissed her. She started the bellows-breathing thing again, which got me excited—her excitement inciting my excitement.

"I like it when you look at me," she said. "It's hot."

Susan had never called me hot. Sometimes she said, "It's hot in here." But I never took that as a compliment.

"You like ska?" she asked, fiddling with the iPod.

"I've never done it, but I'm open to new experiences," I said.

"You're so cute," she said. "You're adorable."

And then suddenly she hiked up the gypsy floral skirt with the black lace and bows at the hem and swung herself over me as if mounting a horse, the motion revealing a complete lack of underdrawers. She blew air out her mouth and preened her neck back and loosened her shirt till I could see that butterfly. She wore an expression that was both sad and beautiful, lorn from absence, from the knowledge that whatever happened between us, it would end badly, that all love ended badly, that we would one day part out of boredom or disgust, or that we would grow old and not be the people we were this minute, or that one or both of us would die and the electric liquid thing that was passing between us would dissipate in the ether. I caught her mood; the moment was worth any loss, any excess. It was worth the sneers of the Somali taxi driver, although, to tell the truth, he wasn't sneering, he was smiling.

Geills lived in a bachelorette apartment in the Wallingfords' basement, no bigger, possibly smaller, than my unit at the rental storage place. The closet had been converted to a bathroom. There was a stove, a refrigerator, a sink, and a foldaway couch that, when extended, fit snugly between the sink cabinet and the facing wall. If you were sleeping, you could not open the door. When we arrived, Frag was in the kitchenette cooking a homecoming meal. I am a private person. I knew I would not be able to use the toilet while Geills was home or Frag was cooking. I also wondered about her relationship with Frag and how things would work out if he wanted to sleep over. There were black-and-white photos tacked to the walls, all pictures of a dog, sometimes alone, sometimes with Geills. Dusty boxes of paperback books climbed the corners of the room. The books on top were pop psychotherapy and diet manuals, guides to a better sex life and animal training how-tos. A camera tripod leaned against the boxes, but there was no sign of a camera. On her bedside table there was a tube of Astroglide, a vibrator, and a copy of *Winnie the Pooh.* I could see clearly we had nothing in common.

I glanced back at the dog pictures, curling at the corners— a vicious, ugly beast with a droll eye. In one of the pictures Geills was kissing the tip of its nose. I suggested that perhaps I should keep my unit at the rental storage place. Frag said he would move to the rental unit. What kind of furniture did I have? He had an open face, an aggressively friendly manner, wore a military fatigue jacket over camouflage pants, T-shirt and combat boots, had a heart and the name *Irma* tattooed on the back of his right hand, and a tic in one eye. To me, he looked schizophrenic, threatening, violent, homeless, and sad. But he shook my hand warmly, asking if I liked red or white, and said he usually cooked Provençal but tonight was a paella the way they made it in Alicante and had I ever been there?

Geills went into the bathroom. I could hear her pee hitting the water in the toilet. Frag took me by the arm and walked me outside, a charming and genteel gesture that at once made me ashamed of myself.

He said, "It really isn't her dog, you know. Not exactly. She got it from a shelter, part pit bull, part greyhound. A street dog from the city. Too wild for her. And she was hitting the booze and doing drugs. It ran away. This was a while ago."

I asked, "What kind of drugs?"

"Oh, the usual kind," he said. "Crystal meth, 'ludes, horse, crack, acid, OxyContin. Mostly booze, though. But also Valium, Percocet. I could go on."

"No, don't," I said.

I said, "I think I'm in over my head." When I said this, I realized it was the sort of thing Susan would say, that I was in over my head.

Frag said, "Is there any other way to be?" He grinned infectiously.

I thought of a dozen sane replies to that, but Geills called from the kitchen, her voice cheerful and pleased with itself, pleased with the world.

Frag said, "Don't fuck this up."

At dinner, she told Frag that she had decided to stop giving him blow jobs because she wanted to be scrupulously loyal to our new love. Frag said he was cool with that. He gave us both a half-dozen assorted pills for dessert and the next thing I knew it was hours later and I was awake on top of Geills with what I believe used to be called a blue-steel boner slapping in and out of her. This went on and on in concert with moans, murmured entreaties, and sighs (and snores—Frag was asleep in some impossibly cramped position on the floor next to the bed). I thought I would never come, but when I did, I felt as if someone were unscrewing the top of my head and red-hot lava was erupting from my eyeballs and my cock had turned inside out and liquefied all at once, flooding her insides with a strange electroluminescence such that I could see the shadows of her ribs and her heart beating beneath her breasts and the blood shifting through her arteries and capillaries and could hear the ancient conversations of tiny one-celled creatures in her gut and the hysterical cheeping of my sperm driving themselves toward her womb.

I said, "I've never felt like this before."

And she whispered, "Drugs get a bad rap."

And then we heard a furious scratching at the door, harsh pants, subterranean whimpers.

"It's the dog," she said urgently.

I thought, Hulking, flame-mouth, blood-drizzling beast, half man, half wolf, size of a small elephant. I started to bark, an insane, pointless, incessant barking in the night. Howling upon her bed. Frag stirred, his eyes snapped open, confused orbs. But she slapped me awake and we rolled the bed up to open the door (Frag's legs became entangled in the bed frame—some obvious discomfort there). And when we finally looked out, the dog was gone. Then the barking began again in the alley beyond the fence, something like my own barks a moment before, assertive, obsessive, insisting on some definite if untranslatable communication, warning us perhaps or demanding food or love or a scratch behind the ear, all maddeningly self-contradictory, for the animal refused to come close enough to receive the attention it desired.

Wrapped in blankets, barefoot despite the hoarfrost that had descended on the city, Geills and I ran after the dog, trailing its barks through alleyways and parking lots, past construction site hoardings, past city parks, past homes where people slept, past dumpsters, dosshouses, cardboard jungles, and rental storage buildings where more people slept—the whole dark and desolate labyrinth of human existence. My feet were bleeding when we returned, and when I woke up she was gone, and Frag was snoring next to me in the bed, with his arm flung over my shoulder.

A few days later, in an act of desperation symbolic of how low I had fallen, I went next door and asked Susan for the loan of a hundred dollars. She said I was in over my head.

I said, "I know. Is there any other way to be?"

She said, "That doesn't sound like something you would say."

And I said, "Maybe fifty dollars?"

I told her about the dog, about Frag, about my burgeoning love for Geills, about the spirit stove explosion and my subsequent dismissal at the college, about the rental unit and my new friends there and the Thursday evening bridge nights, about the Monopoly players at the suicide ward, about the Somali taxi driver, about the novel I had started, writing longhand with a pencil, the old-fashioned way, on paper shopping bags from Safeway.

Susan gasped. It came pouring out of me even as I watched her drawing away, gathering herself in disgust, as if I might contaminate her with my lascivious and libertine ways. Her cheeks were like axe heads; she blushed crimson like a match going up, seemed almost to be suffocating. She lit a cigarette, snapping her lighter nervously, and then lit another without smoking either of them. She combed fingers through her hair and slipped a hand inside her shirt to caress her breast.

I said I was lost but happy. I had nothing. With the money she gave me, I was going to get a tattoo. If she gave me enough, I would get something pierced.

"What?" she gasped again.

"You don't have to live like this either," I said. "You can change."

"You're in over your head," she repeated, handing me the money.

"Geills is teaching me tantric sex," I said, and my wife sighed.

She put her hand inside her pants. She said, "I despise everything you have told me."

And I thought how Proust teaches us that all love resides in anticipation, not the beloved, that love achieved is only on loan, that we are martyrs to our desires, which are endless. I had explained this to Geills between bouts of lovemaking. She said, "Is there a French word for 'Lick my butthole and I'll be yours for life'?"

That day, I borrowed money from five former students before college security evicted me from the campus. I borrowed money from the agent at the rental unit office. Ramon Petunless was hanging around, waiting for me to show up because he needed a recommendation. He was in love with Proust now; he wanted to teach.

I said, "It's common practice for college professors to accept gratuities in exchange for favourable references."

He said, "I didn't know. How much?"

He had an addressed, stamped envelope. I tore the side off a shopping bag and wrote, "On no account accept this man into your program. Keep him away from your wives, your children, and small furry pets. He must be stopped. Do not contact me. I am in hiding from you know who." I sealed it up and handed it back to Ramon to mail.

"I am so grateful, Professor," he said.

"I saved your life," I said.

Then I went to Professor Detweiler's house, Wagner booming in the background, his mousy wife putting dinner on the table, little individual salad bowls at each place full of greens for the bowels. He mentioned the fire again, which I took as fresh evidence of the narrow obsessiveness of the academic mind. He said the logician Zlotsky, who shared my office, had been caught taking photographs of coeds' underpants with a camera attached to a cane. He offered me a large sum to stay away forever.

I said, "Thanks," and, "See you later."

When I got home, Frag was roasting a suckling pig and sipping port while he made up the canapés. The tiny apartment smelled of garlic, ginger, and fennel. The dog was sitting on the couch bed, looking calm, inscrutable, and alert. I recognized it from its photographs.

"I don't know," said Frag. "She was waiting on the porch. I gave her a bowl of kibble. Wait till Geills finds out." He said, "Your wife was here about an hour ago. She had something to ask you. I invited her for dinner. You don't mind, do you?"

I said, "That's still a lot of food for four people."

Frag said, "I invited your friends from the storage place. And some of your students. And Professor Detweiler and his wife, some nurses from the hospital, and the guys from the suicide ward."

He was insanely genial for a man so outwardly menacing. I found it disconcerting, much as I had found all experience disconcerting since I met Geills. She had exposed me to the totally surprising nature of existence, which hitherto had remained hidden from me. She had given me a taste for recklessness. I did not long for my old self, but I was often confused and restless. I was susceptible to minute vibrations from the centre of the universe. The words "rebarbative" and "lobotomy" drifted through my mind like spent arrows coming gradually to rest. The pig's head stared at me through the oven window. The smell of crackling filled our apartment. The dog looked wise, intelligent, and superior.

We waited together, drank port, smoked a joint. People began to drift in for the party. There were five other novelists from the rental storage place, a chess grandmaster, two landscape painters, and a gay new-music composer, along with Ramon Petunless and Akoschka Weatherby. Akoschka Weatherby struck up a conversation with the composer almost at once, revealing herself to be a surprisingly intelligent, darkly beautiful, and even tragic young woman. The dog was alert, ironic, and affectionate. She watched intently and stepped delicately down from the couch to follow me whenever I went to the backyard to pee. Under the moon, the waiting, the gathering of friends, Geills's absence, the dog's cold nose nudging my hand, and the nearly imperceptible vibrations of things seemed strangely prophetic. Frag's Harley gleamed like a chrome statue on the parking pad.

When Susan, my wife, arrived for dinner (along with the Somali cab driver), she seemed hysterical and distant. I could understand this because crowds had always bothered her. She kissed me passionately but absent-mindedly, called me Jean-Luc, which isn't my name, and then noticed the dog. Her eyes widened. She was afraid of dogs. But Frag gave her a hit of that marijuana. She asked if she could smoke a cigarette. Several others were smoking; we were a band of jolly outsiders with a taste for life. She wore a black cocktail dress I had never seen before, hemmed above her knees with one shoulder bare, a thin gold necklace circling her throat. She had put on mascara and eyeliner, too much it seemed, and from either tears or sweat her makeup had begun to run. I thought, She seems vulnerable and brave and beautiful, not the woman she once was nor the woman who once was mine.

Ramon Petunless ushered her away from me to explain how I had saved his life by convincing him to renounce a career in academia. Akoschka Weatherby said I had revealed the true cosmic nature of love to her one day in our Proust seminar. So beautiful and melancholy was her face as she said the words that I knew they must be true. Frag served the canapés and Asti Spumante in tall, elegant glasses and lit candles throughout the apartment.

Nervously, Susan, my wife, tried to make small talk. "Do you need more money?" she asked. "Were you hurt when the spirit stove exploded? I am not much of a critic, but I would like to read your novel."

She seemed bruised, delicate, afraid of rejection. The dog watched, edged closer to Susan. One of the five novelists interrupted, inquiring anxiously if I had found time to look over his revisions. To Susan, my wife, he confided that he had come to depend on my opinion implicitly. Professor Detweiler, appearing tweedy, insignificant, and chastened, asked if I might be available in the coming semester. Some extra funding could certainly be found. There was talk of an endowment for a special chair in Proustian studies.

He said, "You had extraordinary student evaluations."

Frag served the pig, which, as usual, was delicious. We ate off china plates with monogrammed silver cutlery incised with the single letter *F.* The candles burned like a furnace. There was no sign of Geills, but the room was suffused with excitement, anticipation, love, and hope. Conversation centred on books, ideas, art, and complicated chess problems. She rarely spoke, but Susan's eyes were glossy with emotion, her dripping makeup a mask of sadness. Frag played excerpts from Rodrigo's *Concierto de Aranjuez* on an acoustic guitar. I felt swept away with the optimism and poetic beauty of the music. The subtle vibrations of things seemed like the thudding of ancient hill drums and seemed, yes, to be emanating somehow from the dog. The words "rebarbative" and "lobotomy" came to mind and startled me.

Frag said, "Bo, I don't think she's coming back." (My name is not Bo either.)

"Who?" I asked.

He seemed to understand everything.

The dog jumped off the couch and drank thirstily from its bowl, startling Susan, my wife, who leaped into my lap, burying her face against my neck.

Urgently, she whispered, "I want to go away with you."

"I'm not going anywhere," I said.

"I don't want to be your wife any more," she said. "I want to be your lover. I want to throw everything away for you. I want to live in fleabag hotels and work nights as a waitress to support your novel. I want to have your babies. I want you to leave me for mysterious strangers, abandon me on lonely train station platforms, skip out on me in motel rooms with flickering neon lights shining on my bare skin as I lie waiting for you. I want to be lost without you, die for love, find you, and humiliate myself trying to win you back. I don't ever want to go back to what we were."

"But I'm not going anywhere," I said again.

She kissed me hungrily. We had never kissed like that before. I wondered if Geills would mind. But it seemed part of the adventure I was on, the surprising nature of the universe, the aura of love.

She whispered, "I'm not wearing any underwear."

"What changed you so suddenly?" I asked.

"I forgot to do the laundry," she said.

I looked to Frag for advice, but he only shrugged. Ramon Petunless gave me the thumbs-up sign. Akoschka Weatherby blew me a kiss. I thought, I would like to kiss Akoschka Weatherby. Is there any other way to be? I thought. I lifted Susan's dress to see. She had trimmed her pubic hair into a landing strip. There was a fresh tattoo, tiny and elegant, just where her belly met her thigh. The mathematical sign for infinity. Pale skin, never touched by the sun.

Then I knew Geills was never coming back, knew somehow that Geills would never be where the dog was. The dog yawned, scratched speculatively at the door. Someone would let her out soon. I was aware of Geills's mysterious absence and simultaneously the silence, the absence of that pointless, incessant barking that, night after night, had dragged us from our comfortable bed and guided our vain searches.

Frag offered me the keys to the Harley.

"I'm not going anywhere," I said.

But Susan, my wife, gave him an impish wink. The candles flared brilliantly. The brilliant conversation buzzed around us. Already she was ahead of me, leading me into a future, indefinite and innocent.

I thought, Okay. I thought, Affirmative. I thought, Yes. And then I thought again, Yes. Yes.

acknowledgements

The author wishes to acknowledge the support of the Canada Council during the writing of this book.

Many of the stories contained in this collection have appeared in other publications:

"Crown of Thorns" appeared in *The Brooklyn Rail*, April 2011.

"The Sun Lord and the Royal Child" appeared in *Ninth Letter*, Issue No. 13, Spring 2010, and was reprinted in *Best Canadian Stories*, ed. John Metcalf, Oberon Press, Ottawa, 2012.

"A Flame, a Burst of Light" appeared in *The New Quarterly*, No. 118, 2011, and was reprinted in *An Unfinished War*, ed. John B. Lee, Black Moss Press, 2012.

"The Ice Age" was broadcast as "Snow Days" on CBC Radio, *Canada Writes*, December 4, 2012.

"The Poet Fishbein," "Splash," and "Wolven" appeared in *Fence*, Winter 2012-13.

"The Lost Language of Ng" was published in *Fiddlehead*, Summer Fiction Issue, No. 248, 2011.

"A Paranormal Romance" appeared in *The Literarian*, The Center for Fiction, New York, Issue #7, January 19, 2012.

"Shameless" appeared in *The Brooklyn Rail*, December-January 2007.

"Uncle Boris Up in a Tree" appeared in *Descant,* 40th Anniversary Issue, No. 153, 2011.

"Savage Love" appeared in *CNQ, Canadian Notes & Queries*, No. 74, 2008.

"Pointless, Incessant Barking in the Night" appeared in *Best Canadian Stories*, ed. John Metcalf, Oberon Press, Ottawa, 2009, and was reprinted in *Descant*, No. 148, Spring, 2010.